MW01228118

Praise for Heir of Evil

In "Heir of Evil" there is not a single page that is tedious. The action is fast and each word, each movement and each gesture of the characters has a meaning of great importance with which the argument cannot be dispensed with. I greatly admire the author's talent, imagination and historical accuracy.

-Billy Peña, Book critic

The premise of Heir of Evil is in itself a very interesting and imaginative idea.

-Reynaldo Yanez, author

It's credible as a story worthy of the secret archives of the US government, one of those that governments always deny that happened.

-Bladimir Burgos, author

HEIR OF EVIL

By J. H. Bográn

To Ligia, Daniel, Sebastián, and Gustavo

HEIR OF EVIL

By J. H. Bográn

CHAPTER ONE

Berlin, April 28, 1945

Blondi raised her head, posed her saddened brown eyes on her master for the last time, then died. She had been a faithful, noble and elegant German shepherd who had delighted her master's guests with the tricks for which she had been trained.

The air in the courtyard of the damaged Chancellery became impregnated with a strong smell of almonds. The eyes of the man, kneeling next to the shepherd, were sad, melancholic. Despite having sentenced hordes of men, women and children to death, watching his dog dying troubled him. Adolf Hitler distrusted the efficiency of the cyanide pills issued to all the tenants of the bunker. He chose this purpose for his pet to quiet his doubts. Plus, it was better that Blondi died by his own hand. In his mind, he had the firm conviction that the dog would have preferred a send-off at the hands of her master instead of those damn Russians.

He got up slowly and walked a few steps towards the secret entrance of the shelter located under the Chancellery in the German capital. His assistant, Otto Günsche, and the few soldiers around him felt overwhelmed, not knowing what to say. How could they comfort their leader? When they were descending the stairs, the Russians' guns could be heard in the distance as they riddled Berlin with unparalleled fury. The city would soon fall into the hands of the Soviets. The Germans knew they had lost the war, but none had the courage to say it out loud, much less in front of the Führer.

His private office, located adjacent to the map room, was a rectangular room lit by two lamps situated between the desk and a bureau attached to the end wall. On the right an immense map of Europe and Africa showed the position of the troops of the Third Reich. The area that until recently covered from the Urals to the coast of Portugal, was now limited to what was the original border of Germany before the start of the war in 1939. France had been liberated. Italy defeated, and his fascist dictator Mussolini killed on the streets like a common dog. The troops who were mere miles away from entering victoriously into Cairo one year ago, were no longer distinguishable in the upper part of Africa. Japan was the only one still fighting in the Pacific. The fascist Axis was coming to an end.

In the center of the room, a majestic mahogany desk was buried under hundreds of papers that demanded the signature of the owner of the unoccupied black leather chair. In front of the desk were two chairs for visitors, one of which was occupied by the Führer's doctor.

The other furniture in the room was comprised of a sofa and a coffee table for informal visits.

Seeing Hitler enter, the doctor stood up and raised his right arm with the dignified salute of proud Nazi Germany.

"Heil Hitler!"

"Any news, Hoffman?" The leader asked as he indicated to the others to leave the room.

"Yes, sir," replied the doctor.

The doctor waited to have the complete attention of his interlocutor. Hitler stopped before going around the desk, raised his head and fixed his gaze on the doctor's eyes.

"Fraulein Braun is pregnant. She is about nine weeks."

Hearing this, the Führer flinched, a slight smile crossing his lips. Hoffman could see a glint in his eyes, which the doctor thought was the light at the end of the tunnel. He did not know the real reasons for Hitler's joy, so he assumed it was for future fatherhood. The old doctor was wrong.

* * *

A few hours earlier, Eva Braun laid beside Hitler in a windowless room, deep in the bunker, the last refuge. The walls had no decoration. Their color was the same grayish natural reinforced cement, a fortification that guaranteed security, but not comfort.

Nausea had awakened her that morning. At near five o'clock in the morning, she got up hurriedly to rush to the bathroom. She knelt on the floor and spilled the contents of her stomach in the toilet. Her throat burned from the gastric acid, and her heart beat very fast. Eva felt tears roll down her cheeks.

Hitler came to the door. "How are you feeling?"

"Not well. It must be something I ate," she said hoarsely.

The Führer watched her closely. She was thinner than usual. Her pale complexion, eyes a deep red at that time, were surrounded by a black shadow.

"I want you to see Doctor Hoffman. I'll send him later."

"It's nothing, really."

But Eva noticed something in the eyes of the one she had followed to Hell itself. The determination was there, and she understood how useless it would be to try to persuade him. She nodded and stood to return to the room.

True to his word Hitler demanded the sexagenarian Dr. Hoffman to visit her. At first, he asked her a series of routine questions, took her pulse, listened to her heart and lungs. He told her that despite the apparent insufficient weight, she showed good health. He then ordered her to lie down on the bed and remove her underwear. Eva felt uncomfortable. Sitting on the edge of the bed, she did not move a muscle. The doctor smiled and sat next to her.

"Do not worry," he said, "I'll explain everything I do."

Eva watched the white-haired doctor with his round glasses that were about to slide over his nose. Hoffman pushed them back with his right hand while smiling benevolently.

Although Eva was still uncomfortable, the doctor inspired enough confidence to obey him.

Hoffman sat on a bench by the bed and began to explain what he wanted to do while putting a glove on his hand. As he spoke, partly to distract her, the doctor put his index finger into the vaginal area and felt the cervix. Eva felt the discomfort and saw the doctor frown.

The doctor went to the bathroom to wash his hands. Upon returning he found Eva sitting on the bed, obviously distressed. Her face showed her fear. The doctor returned to his position on the bench next to the bed and asked, "When was your last period, Fräulein?"

"I do not know," she said. She thought for a moment, then added, "Mid-March, I think.

The doctor sighed with a smile which calmed Braun.

"Your illness will end approximately in January, Fräulein. Congratulations, the Führer will soon have his first child."

She smiled, relieved. The news of a new life developing within a mother is well received, even in the worst circumstances.

* * *

Upon hearing the news, Hitler launched into a frenetic activity. The Führer met behind closed doors with his most trusted man. Someone who would never appear in history books because he always advised from the shadows, never the center of attention. Very few people knew of his existence.

Helmut Dietz, excited about the news, formed a long-term plan and presented it to his boss.

"Are you sure it's going to work?"

"The plan is flexible. If it fails in its first attempt, we can try it again later."

"There isn't much time left. When can you have everything ready?"

"Money is not a problem. We have it ready, hidden in accounts in Switzerland that only I have access to," Helmut said.

"But you will not live forever. We need someone younger."

"Werner, my oldest son, is thirteen years old. I think he can serve us."

Hitler leaned back in his chair, sighed. He observed his companion who held a cigar in his right hand, playing with his fingers. The Führer, who was a health-conscious vegetarian and did not smoke, extended his regimen to his relatives who were not allowed to smoke in his presence either. He knew that Helmut would not dare light up in his office, but he was disturbed for a moment by the fact that he had it so close at hand. A minute passed before he spoke again.

"We need someone who looks like Eva."

"For what?"

"If people think that she survived the bunker, she will always be watched, even arrested and the news would be known."

"But Dr. Hoffman knows it."

Hitler shook his head in a symbol of denial. "He was sacrificed for the good of the Third Reich."

Dietz smiled. "Then only you, Eva and I know about it."

The Führer nodded.

"Das ist recht! I have the papers ready. But we have to change Fräulein's appearance."

"With surgery?" Hitler asked.

"Impossible. In her current state, she cannot be anesthetized. But she must look different. Change her hair, do not use makeup. Change her name."

"How about Helen Brown, as the Americans write it?"

Dietz explained how he had secured a series of papers that credited the bearer as a Swiss national. All that was needed was to fill out the name. It was his supreme escape plan. However, he explained it to the Führer very delicately to prevent him from thinking he was a traitor to the party. He revealed that he already had a place in the United States where Eva could give birth out of public scrutiny. Hitler paid close attention, and, in the end, he praised the work of Helmut. Together they worked out the final points to the plan.

Hitler understood at that moment that the only way for his ideals to survive and for the plan they were plotting to work, he would have to be defeated before the world. But surrendering to the allies was too much for his pride. The world would not see him humiliated in defeat. He'd rather die.

One of his last arrangements occurred on April 30. Hitler formalized their relationship by marrying Eva Braun so that his son could be legitimate. Then they smuggled her to America.

Helmut entered the office at about four in the afternoon, followed by a tall, thin woman with blond hair who could be mistaken for Eva Braun at a distance. Hitler was sitting on the sofa, Günschen standing in front of him.

"Do you understand the instructions? There should be no trace, my body will not become anyone's trophy."

"Yes, I understand. I have prepared the place and the fuel to incinerate it." He answered, his face tense at the seriousness of the arrangements he had just received.

Hitler nodded. "Well, wait outside for fifteen minutes, then carry out your orders."

Günschen saluted, raising his arm and left the office, pulling the door closed behind him.

"It's her?"

"Yes. Everything is ready."

Helmut guided the woman to the sofa where she fell heavily. Hitler came around the desk and sat on the other end. He noticed the lost look of the woman and looked up at Helmut.

Helmut shrugged. "She's drugged. It was the only way," he explained bluntly.

Dietz took two pills of cyanide from his coat pocket and placed one into the woman's mouth. She offered no resistance as she quickly died. He then produced a revolver that he placed on the table. After a few seconds, his body contracted in a spasm and his face turned into a grimace of horror before he died.

Hitler watched silently as the macabre spectacle unfolded. Helmut turned towards him and realized that his turn had arrived. The Führer pulled his own revolver from his belt and handed it to Dietz.

"Has to be with my own weapon," he said as he took out his dose of cyanide, brought it to his mouth without saying a final word.

Dietz, with the revolver in his hand, pointed it at the Führer's right temple. The poison was taking effect and a grimace of terror like that of the woman gripped his face.

"Auf wiedersehen, mein Führer," he said before pulling the trigger. He put the gun away and left the room.

* * *

San Francisco Bay, 1976

The sun began to descend on the Pacific, turning the sea into endless shades of orange. The bay was full of sailboats entering and leaving the high seas. About two kilometers from the marina was a lonely anchored yacht. In the stern were several people, all dressed in black. In front of them, a priest was saying the last prayers. In his hands, he held an urn, chest high. Among those present was a six-year-old boy, crying. He didn't understand what was happening around him. No one had been able to explain to him why his father had left. Nobody could explain to him that his father's body was so mutilated, in the car accident, that cremation had been the only solution. The child's mother, standing behind him, was crying inconsolably. She felt abandoned, without support. When the priest finished the prayers, he prepared to throw the ashes into the sea.

"In nomine patris, et filii, et spiriti sancti, Amen."

Ceremoniously, he uncapped the urn and threw the ashes. To the boy it seemed like a small gray cloud that the wind immediately scattered, taking the particles to the sea as well as to the horizon. At that moment, the child's mother gave a cry of distress and fainted.

* * *

Paris, 1998

"The Mona Lisa is missing! I repeat: the Mona Lisa is missing!" screamed the frantic man on his radio.

His heart pounded in his chest as he witnessed the impossible: somebody broke into the Louvre and stole the most famous painting in the world! Worst of all, as head of security, the responsibility was all on him.

André Belzeaux had worked at the museum for the previous seven years, serving the last two as Chief of Security during the day shift. Every morning, the man in his mid-forties walked half the length of the museum, looking for things out of place. Even when the building is protected with several hundred strategically located cameras, he enjoyed his strolls. An amateur art connoisseur, he befriended the museum's curator. They met every morning at nine to have coffee and croissants, sitting in different areas and discuss nothing but art.

When André arrived on Tuesday morning, he reached the chamber where DaVinci's Mona Lisa was protected behind thick glass plates. He gaped in awe at the empty space. After calling in on his radio, the alarm went off in the private area; heavy metal doors locking nothing but air inside behind them.

André ran to the security headquarters where he could monitor the cameras. He entered the room and watched one of his men turning dials on his console zooming in to the missing frame.

"Should we call the police?" asked another man sitting behind a small desk. He already had the phone in his hand.

"No, let's try to locate it here first," André said after he quickly considered his options.

The idea that he might lose his job didn't even cross his mind, neither the fact that he wanted to keep it quiet. The reason he delayed calling the police was a more practical one: He knew and trusted all the staff working that morning. Letting the police know would mean filling the building with strangers.

He paced behind the ten consoles that helped monitor the museum. His men were quickly clicking and turning the cameras around the museum to find any clue to what happened.

"Monsieur," the one sitting in the far corner called.

André approached the man's workstation as he pointed with his index finger at the screen.

"There's a strange object covering one side of the small pyramid at the entrance," he said.

The ceiling of the entrance to the museum was shaped like an inverted pyramid, the tip reaching down, almost touching the tip of a smaller similarly shaped object rising from the ground.

The camera zoomed in on the west face of the pyramid. The sides were perfectly aligned to the cardinal points.

"Yes, I see it!" said André.

He squinted hard to see the object in the monitor. The glass surface seemed covered with a black cloth. But he could not ascertain what it was. He walked back to the door where he had entered less than five minutes before.

"I'll check it out. You keep searching!" he said as he closed the door after him.

André rushed to the lobby. When he arrived, two other guards were already there, hunched over the pyramid. Neither dared to touch anything.

His chest heaving, the chief of security pulled the black flannel cloth from the pyramid. His jaw dropped when he saw the missing piece of art leaning against the small triangular facade. He noticed a white piece of paper taped to the left side of the frame.

The three men traded a look of surprise and bewilderment, then André bent to read the printed text of the letter written in French:

Dear Mr. Belzeaux:

First, I apologize for this crude manner of pointing out the flaws in the system used to protect this priceless painting. I took the liberty of listing them below for your review, along with a few humble suggestions in how to improve them.

I didn't receive any help from your guards, and I commend them for the loyalty shown by the ones I tried to bribe.

Let me reassure you that my intentions are honorable. I beg of you to take better care of the Mona Lisa as I doubt any of my colleagues would return it as I have.

Sincerely,
The Falcon

CHAPTER TWO

New York, autumn of 1999

The carpet of leaves covered the paths of Central Park in yellow, orange and gray tones. However, the natural spectacle went unnoticed by the inhabitants of the city, who rushed to their jobs in the Big Apple or who returned to their homes in the city that never sleeps.

Within ten minutes of starting a typical Friday activity, Wall Street had legions of stockbrokers willing to fight for a few dollars more. In the corridors of the Stock Exchange, these new soldiers had replaced the rifle and bayonet by pen and notebook. The Great War campaigns had morphed into theories of the Free Market. Buy, sell, change, wait for the moment, and seize the opportunity. The levels of adrenaline that are reached on any given day in the stock exchange matched that of any battle of yesteryear.

Johan Trading Corporation paid an annuity granting him the right to use one of the box offices to conduct its negotiations. Inside this office was a tall, thin man with black hair cut in the traditional style and light brown eyes. He wore an impeccable navy-blue suit, tailored to fit. A white shirt and red tie completed the outfit. Oscar Brown was, at twenty-nine, one of the best in the business. In just four years he became vice president of the company that occupied one of the most important positions for the multi-million-dollar volumes handled in the stock market. He radiated such magnetism that it was said to have the gift of turning a Jew into a Catholic.

Standing next to the window, he heard the bell to start the activity. Pandemonium broke out. Anyone who did not have a trained eye could not understand what was happening. Oscar retreated to his desk and observed the trends on his computer screen.

The objective of the day was to observe the behavior of orange juice. The year before, Florida suffered the coldest winter of the last fifty years. The harvests had suffered a million-dollar loss and the price in the international market had reached exorbitant figures. As the next winter approached, all eyes lifted expectantly toward the sky.

"Linda, get me the forecasts for the next week, okay?"

Linda Mathews was his personal assistant, late thirties, a widow, and a jewel of a professional. She knew the needs of her boss and it was common for her to get ahead of his orders.

"Here you. are. The second page contains the satellite photos," she said as she put a bundle of papers on the desk.

"Why do I want photos?" Oscar protested.

"I thought the presentation would look better with photos and not just boring graphs."

"They're going to believe I'm giving the damned weather report!" he said, indignantly.

"Well, that's exactly what you will do."

Oscar smiled. She was right. His meeting with the board of directors was in a couple hours and it was imperative that he give them the timely report to convince them that the investment of so much capital in orange juice was safe.

Brown settled down to calmly read the reports as he alternated his attention to the screen of his computer, where the graphics appeared. Linda also made sure the blue cup at the end of the desk was filled with fresh coffee.

At ten thirty the trend was on the rise. Oscar headed to the elevator. He went down to the basement, walked out through the parking lot and crossed the street to the building opposite. The main entrance to the stock exchange building was on the other side of the block, but the parking lot was in the back. The building where Johan had his offices was across the street from the parking lot, so it was easier to get out that way. The only ones who walked into the building through the parking lot were Johan's employees.

* * *

The sniper on the roof lay on his stomach holding his .223 caliber rifle. He hid under a thin blanket in shades of gray that provided camouflaged from the eyes of any curious on-lookers in another building and the police or news helicopters that circulated incessantly in the Big Apple. Luckily the climate lent itself to this type of trickery. During the summer the heat would have been unbearable. But now, in mid-autumn, with his long hair tied in a tail to keep it in place, the covering did not cause sweat to stain the green Polo shirt, which highlighted the color of his eyes, nor the Levi jeans he wore.

The assassin mocked his profession by traveling under the pseudonym David Graves, claiming it was to the grave where he sent his victims. His other passport had the name of Robert I. Prescott, symbolizing with his initials "Rest in Peace" that is customarily written on gravestones. Entering the army of his native country at seventeen, he was treated harshly by his superiors and companions because of the association of the bad luck redheads bring. However, his expertise with weapons was exceptional and he was soon recruited by the SAS, or special operations division of the British Army. During the war in the Persian Gulf in '92, his patrol was assigned the mission of locating and assassinating the Iraqi president, but all efforts to locate the target were useless and the order was canceled before it was executed. Once he returned to his country, Graves requested a discharge and began renting his services to the highest bidder. Eight years later he had an enviable reputation and although the price depended to a large extent on the objective, the average was a million dollars per job.

That amount was being charged on this occasion, although his client had been very specific in making his proposal: Do not kill

Oscar Brown. The name of his target was no secret. He was a vice president at a major stock exchange company on Wall Street.

Finally, Brown came walking out of the parking lot as Graves had been told would happen. Closing one eye, he fixed the other against the telescope mounted on the weapon. With the magnification of the lens, he could watch the parking lot door more than thirty stories away as if it were a few meters away.

"The subject just left." He reported through the microphone secured with a clip to his shirt.

Accustomed to working alone, Graves hated to be communicating with that stranger on the radio. He had received the frequency with which he should connect, wait and warn when acquiring the target. During the three hours he'd waited, he only lowered the weapon once, to use an empty plastic canister to relieve his bladder. It did not take more than a minute before he resumed his post.

"Right. Proceed with the plan." He heard the answer through the earphone in his right ear.

Graves knew enough about the set up to know that his client was close, maybe in some nearby office where he could monitor all the action. As a good professional, he determined to do his job. The assassin took aim at the predefined target, held his breath and pulled the trigger.

The bullet traveled its course at a speed one thousand two hundred meters per second, broke a street lamp, to end up embedded in a wall to the left of the target. The shooter watched through his telescope as Oscar stopped, and turned in surprise towards the lamp. He stared at it as if asking what had happened. Then he shrugged, checked both sides of the street and crossed to his office.

"Mission accomplished. Although I do not think the subject has noticed yet."

"He'll know later. The rest of your money is being transferred to the account at this time."

Graves did not understand the purpose of the exercise he had just completed. It was the first time that they hired him to leave someone alive, although the pay was good. The man got on his knees, dismantled his weapon, folded the blanket, and put everything in a black backpack.

"It's too bad this rifle will end up at the bottom of the Hudson River," he said stubbornly.

He got up and slung his backpack over his shoulder as he left the roof.

* * *

When Oscar entered the opulent lobby, the receptionist rose to greet him and gave him a stack of messages. Oscar took them and read them hurriedly while he went to the conference room.

"And that gentlemen, was the forecast for the weekend," Oscar joked when he finished his presentation a few hours later.

All the partners around the table laughed. It was true that Oscar had given them a report with the weather forecast. However, the reason was not to plan the annual picnic for employees in sunny Florida. The company Sunny Valley was dedicated to the production and distribution of orange juice. It was the third largest company in the country in its field, and when they became interested in making their company public, they looked at Johan Trading to handle the transactions, with Brown being the facilitator of the deal.

At the head of the table sat a tough man, over sixty years old who had been in Johan's presidency for the last fifteen years, since his father died. Patrick Johan was satisfied with his protégé's work. He had to convince many people before he was able to give the vice presidency to a person under thirty years of age. But with this news, there was no doubt that the election had been successful.

"Well, gentlemen, without more points on the agenda, I think we're done for today."

"How marvelous!" said one of those present "I will finally arrive home early on a Friday!"

"You can't leave. It's only three in the afternoon," Johan said, smiling.

The jocular comment was well received by the members as they rose from the table and, one by one, marched out. Oscar was aware of what he had just achieved before the board of directors. He stayed according to the wishes of his boss and mentor.

"You did well to stay, Oscar."

"You always have last-minute comments. So, I thought, we better get it over with at once."

"Not today. But I wanted to wish you luck tonight."

"Excuse me?" Oscar said, surprised.

"I know very soon there will be a district attorney changing her last name to Brown," Patrick replied, smiling.

"How do you know that?"

"It's my job to know everything that happens in this company. Also, your decisions reflect on my judgment of appointing you vice president."

The tone was affable, but Oscar understood that the scrutiny for his appointment also extended to the decisions he made in his personal life.

"Thanks. See you on Monday, Mr. Johan," Oscar said as he left the room.

He did not feel bothered at all. On the contrary, his plans were to make that evening memorable. Assuming she accepted the proposal, of course.

* * *

Oscar was driving his luxurious green sedan to the restaurant where he was scheduled to meet Nora Miller. While waiting at a traffic light, he took from his pocket a small box lined with black velvet. He opened it to observe, for the umpteenth time, the engagement ring. This was the big day: he had received confirmation of his work, and now he could commit in the long term.

The light changed to green. The young executive sighed and closed the box, put it on the passenger seat, and then began to accelerate. His peripheral vision caught something to the left. He turned in time to see the front of a vehicle approaching at full speed. Oscar heard the impact before his body reacted to the blow. Then everything went dark.

The pain seared into his body before he fully regained consciousness. Intense pain, nothing else existed. It was isolated, but with an unbearable slowness, Oscar determined it was in his head, arm, and left leg. He opened his eyes and the penetrating fluorescent light of the hospital accentuated the suffering. He closed his eyes again and tried to open them slowly until they became accustomed to the light.

"Mr. Brown, do you hear me?" A male voice said.

"Yes."

"You know, you were extremely lucky that your vehicle had side airbags."

Oscar suddenly envisioned the salesman who suggested the side bags; heard that voice that said: "They are not standard in this model, but I suggest that, for only two hundred dollars more, we include them. You will not regret it."

"It was not my idea," he said aloud. At that moment he managed to determine the man he spoke with was a doctor, dressed in traditional light green attire, with stethoscope around his neck.

"If I may, I suggest you thank the man after you leave the hospital."

Oscar sighed, his memory beginning to work. Images of the street came to mind, then a noise to his left. He turned to see a vehicle approaching at full speed. There was something in the front glass. His mind registered the image, but his common sense chose to ignore it. After all, it could not have been a swastika.

Or was it?

"Fortunately, you don't have any fractured bones, either in the arm or in the leg. But there are minor cuts, bruises, things like that," the doctor said in a professional and courteous tone.

"So, will I be fine?"

"Yes. You will have to stay here for a couple of days, but on Sunday afternoon you can go home."

"If there's no other choice. What a fun weekend!" He managed to say.

"Did you have an important commitment?"

"I was just going to a restaurant to propose to my girlfriend," Oscar said.

"Don't worry. You'll have enough time to celebrate later."

There were several questions Oscar needed to ask. He didn't understand why, but he had an insatiable need to know.

"How did I get here?"

"An ambulance brought you. As I understood, a passing car called 911 and reported the accident. The car that hit you fled. Tomorrow the police will come to ask you some questions. In fact, they wanted to do it today, but the patient comes first. I told them you would receive them tomorrow."

Oscar nodded, but the pain was getting stronger and he asked the doctor if they could give him something to alleviate the growing discomfort. The doctor checked the file at the foot of the bed to verify what medications had already been administered and promised to send the nurse with something to help him rest.

Brown was left alone in the room. He could see the television in front of him, but the remote control was out of reach. So, he had to settle for sighing and waiting.

Finally, the nurse entered the room. She approached and put an injection into the tube that was already inserted in the vein of Oscar's right arm. He thanked her as he began to feel an intense heat that moved through his entire body.

He was in a private room. To his right was a window with the curtains closed. In the back corner, there was a door that, he supposed, led to the bathroom. The walls were bare, there were no paintings or other decoration. To his left was the door that led to the corridor, through which, at that moment, he could see the back of the nurse who closed it.

* * *

In the morning, the pain returned with a vengeance, but it was relieved by another timely visit from the nurse. This time the medicine was not so strong as to make him sleep, but enough to make him comfortable throughout the morning.

At eight o'clock, they brought him breakfast. The nurse offered to help him eat, but Oscar preferred to do it alone.

"Mr. Brown, you have both arms immobilized: the left one by the blow and the right one by the intravenous tube. Let me help you," the nurse said before removing the cover of the plate.

The room was infused with a pleasant smell of food. Oscar realized he hadn't eaten since the previous day's lunch. Hunger won the battle over pride and Oscar prepared to be fed like a baby.

"Could I sit up a little?" He asked the nurse.

The nurse took the control of the electric bed and lifted the back. Oscar sensed the movement, but his arm began to hurt. He moaned, and the nurse stopped. She adjusted the pillows to make him feel better.

At the end of the breakfast came a serious looking guy, tall, dressed in black jeans and a plaid shirt, somewhat obese, but his muscular arms denoting an athletic body in the past. Too many donuts, Oscar thought, sarcastically.

"Good morning, Mr. Brown. I'm Sergeant Frank Hagen. I work with the Metropolitan Police. I need to ask you some questions for the report." The tone was polite but authoritative.

"As you like," he turned to the nurse who was frowning in disapproval.

The interrogation was not very extensive: to find out if Oscar was insured, what was the direction he was going, and if he saw the license plate of the vehicle. The first two responses left Hagen satisfied, but not the third.

"Everything happened very fast, Sergeant. I only managed to see that it was a big car, possibly a truck or an all-terrain vehicle."

"Anything else you can add?"

Oscar sighed. He did not know whether to tell the policeman what he thought he saw in the glass. In the end, he decided to do it.

"Sergeant, I saw something, but I'm not sure. You're going to think I'm crazy.

"Don't worry, Mr. Brown. Just tell me what you saw."

"Well, I thought I saw a big Nazi flag on the glass. You know, red and with the black swastika in the middle."

"I know the flag perfectly, Mr. Brown. My parents managed to escape from Germany before the outbreak of World War II."

His face reflected his indecision, then added, "Even so, they were arrested and sent to a prison camp here in the United States."

His frankness took Oscar by surprise. After a few seconds pondering what he had just heard, he was consumed by doubt.

"And still you became a policeman?"

"Yes, I thought it was better to clean from inside. I can't stand injustice, and I have fought all my life against stereotypes and prejudices."

At that moment the door opened with such force that it hit the back wall. Both men turned in amazement to find a woman in the doorway. The dark patches under her eyes and the glassy red color betrayed that she had been crying all night. Seeing Oscar lying on the bed, she went to his side.

Brown felt the silky brown hair of his girlfriend while listening to her softly weeping on his shoulder.

"Oscar, forgive me. I didn't know what happened to you. I thought you had forgotten again. And then, and ..." she managed to say between sobs.

"Don't worry, Nora," he said as he kissed her on the head, "it wasn't that bad."

"Good to see you, Ms. Miller," Hagen said

Nora raised her head and stared at the policeman.

"I'm Sergeant Hagen from the Metro. We met at the courthouse. Don't you remember me?" He asked affably.

Nora's expression changed from surprise to realization as her eyes showed a special glow. Knowing her, Oscar supposed that she had remembered all the details of the case from which she had met Hagen.

"The Medina case?"

"I know that you were supporting the prosecutor in the final part of the trial. At least, justice was done."

"Yes, that living evil will not hit his wife anymore."

"That was six months ago," Hagen said, explaining to Brown.

"Yes, very good. Sergeant Hagen, please excuse the rudeness, I'm a little upset. But why are you here?"

"The car that hit Mr. Brown fled, I don't think we'll find it, but I have to do a routine investigation. You understand that, right?"

"He escaped. I didn't know that." She turned towards Oscar. "Oh heavens, forgive me for not having been here last night. I did not realize until now."

"Don't worry. I'm sorry I stood you up," Oscar said.

Frank Hagen stood to say goodbye, leaving his card in case Oscar remembered something else.

Oscar and Nora were left alone in the room. She still could not get over the fact that she had been angry with Oscar all night, thinking he had forgotten her, only to discover the truth in the morning. It was very overwhelming for the assistant district attorney.

At lunchtime, Nora fed Oscar, who remembered why he had invited her at the restaurant.

The ring! He did not know where it was, or if it had been taken out of the vehicle.

A proposal without a ring wouldn't be very convincing, although Brown had the perfect excuse. The best part of the case was that it was true. However, he decided not to propose to Nora there in the hospital. He was convalescing, and she had suffered all night. It would not be fair to either of them.

By afternoon, the room was full of flowers. Patrick Johan happened to visit along with his wife. When he saw no ring on Nora's finger, he remained silent. But they exchanged glances with Oscar, and he was sure Patrick could figure out what had happened.

CHAPTER THREE

The following Tuesday after the accident, Oscar decided to return to work. When he arrived, Linda told him about the mountain of messages he had to answer. After traversing the party that greeted him at the door, he managed to reach his desk. He set the crutches aside and dropped heavily into his black leather chair. He felt exhausted. He and Linda had developed a system for placing papers on the desk, so Oscar could at a glance know where to look for the most urgent to be resolved. On this day the stack of urgent issues was higher. He sighed and began to read the papers.

It had not been two minutes when the phone rang. Oscar looked up and pressed the intercom button.

"Linda, if you keep interrupting me with phone calls I'll never get through these papers."

"I know, but the call is from the president of Gewinn, Werner Dietz."

Oscar was surprised. Gewinn was the largest company in Europe. Johan was mere pocket change compared to the operations of the old continent. Being so big, it was impossible not to know them, much less not having had to deal with them at some point. Oscar had talked with Gewinn the previous year when a client wanted to invest in Europe, but the deal was never finalized.

Werner Dietz must be one of the busiest men in the world. What could he want to talk about with Oscar? His mind was blank. He took the call with certain reservations.

"Good Morning."

"Good afternoon, Oscar." The voice on the other end of the line was grave and full of seriousness. "This is Werner Dietz."

He knows who I am?

"Of course, Mr. Dietz. How may I help you?"

"Thanks, but first I want to know how you are. I heard about your accident. Alright, I hope." Werner spoke the language almost perfectly. There was only a glimmer of a German accent in certain words.

"No broken bones, but many bandages and bruises. For now, I'm on crutches, but I'll survive. Thank you for asking."

"Don't mention it. Listen, I'm in New York this week and I want to invite you to dinner. On Thursday, if you have no other plans, of course.

This took Oscar even more by surprise. He reviewed his schedule and saw that on Thursday he had nothing. Well, nothing work related. He had invited Nora to dinner. Kneeling with crutches would be more complicated, but he thought that if he delayed any longer, he might lose the courage.

"Thank you very much, Mr. Dietz, but I have another commitment that day.

"Are you sure?"

"Yes. Very sure. It's something personal that I have planned."

"This would be good for you, Oscar. You know I'm not the kind of person who offers things twice."

The last comment set off an alarm in his head. Oscar was not used to being spoken to in ultimatums. Calmly, he tried to analyze the situation.

Werner Dietz, one of the richest men in the world, calls a perfect stranger to invite him to dinner. He must have been a man who rarely heard the word no. Moreover, the last sentence implied that he wanted to offer something. Oscar doubted it was just dinner. Is it maybe some work in Gewinn? That could be. Better be sure ...

"Mr. Dietz, you're right. It's a discourtesy on my part. You come from Europe and invite me to dinner. How could I refuse you? Thank you."

"And your personal matter?"

"It was a romantic dinner with my girlfriend. I think I can renegotiate it for a weekend at the beach."

"I would accept it."

Both men laughed, but the arrangement was made.

"I'll see you on Thursday at eight o'clock at the Four Seasons."

"Perfect, Sir. I'll be there."

When he hung up the phone, Oscar became thoughtful. It was too early to get excited about Gewinn's proposal. The truth was that Dietz only talked about dinner.

At half past five in the afternoon, Linda came to his office to say goodbye. She was used to letting her boss work late, but she thought that maybe this day she would want to leave early.

"We'll see you tomorrow, Linda. Don't worry, Nora will pick me a little later."

When his fiancée arrived at seven o'clock for him, the "urgent" pile was no longer the tallest on the desk. Oscar still could not drive, and even if he could, his vehicle was unusable for urban transport.

Nora Miller still looked like her conscience was eating at her for believing Oscar had stood her up and seemed determined to help as much as possible without protest. She was an attractive woman, of Oscar's age, never married, and in fact, her profession as a prosecutor was her priority.

Oscar met her by chance one day in the park while he was walking his dog. She was with her sister and her three-year-old nephew. The dog began to play with the little one and Oscar came running after him apologizing for the forwardness of the dog.

Her sister made the comment that apparently the dog never left the house. When Oscar admitted his work addiction, the sister concluded that they would be the perfect couple. Oscar and Nora began to talk about their professions, what they liked and what they detested.

Within two months, they had built a strong relationship. Soon after, Oscar asked Nora's nephew to take care of his dog. Because of work, he kept the dog locked in the apartment most of time. The dog would be happier with the boy.

Two years later, Oscar was ready for the next step. But this would be the second time he'd have to postpone his plans.

On the way to Oscar's apartment, he told her about the call he had received. She was surprised and was not bothered at all because of the cancellation of dinner plans. On the contrary, she was very excited about the appointment and the trip to Florida that Oscar promised her.

The next day, Linda made reservations at a Miami hotel. They would leave on Friday night and return on Sunday. It was not a long time, but it would be enough to take a break from the accelerated life that both led.

* * *

The Four Seasons was one of the most famous restaurants in New York, as well as one of the most expensive. Its clientele was exclusive. Oscar arrived at the restaurant a little before eight. The Maitre'd told him that Mr. Dietz was already waiting for him, and he led him to the table.

As Brown approached, his host rose to meet him. The handshake was firm, unusually firm for someone of Werner's age. The man radiated power. They took their seats and the waiter took Oscar's order. He already had Dietz's.

"Something to drink?" the waiter asked.

"Scotch on the rocks, please," Oscar said.

The waiter nodded and withdrew. Oscar turned to Werner who was had a smile.

"We share good taste in liquor."

"It looks that way. But someone told me you only drink Blue Label."

"It's the best!"

The dinner conversation focused on several recent cases from Wall Street. Both took care not to say anything that could be considered illegal in the environment in which they worked. The food, as expected, was excellent. By the time of dessert was served, Oscar began to lower his guard a little. At that moment, Werner took the opportunity to surprise him.

"I have followed your career for some time, Oscar, and I think you can be very useful in Gewinn. I want you to work for me."

The declaration left Oscar speechless. After a full minute, Oscar was able to respond.

"I'm surprised by the offer. I mean, I perhaps expected something like this. It is not normal for the president of such a large company to invite a person to dinner without having any kind of agenda. But…"

Werner smiled. "I would have been very disappointed if you told me you did not expect something like this. This confirms my intuition about you."

"What's the offer?"

"Now we are talking! President of operations. Your only boss would be me. And the board of directors, of course. Your salary will be three times what you earn now. And believe me when I tell you, I know what you earn."

Werner allowed a minute for Oscar to assimilate what he had just said.

"Well, what's your answer?"

Oscar's mind was suddenly filled with idea that collided with one another. The salary package he had negotiated with Johan Tradings was very good, one of the best. However, three times that amount meant millions. One of the many ideas told him that it was useless to think so much. In the end, his only reaction was to nod.

"You understand you need to move to Frankfurt, right?

Oscar nodded, but he had not really thought about this. Suddenly, his thoughts drifted away from the money and focused on his girlfriend. Nora Miller was a lawyer in the United States. She probably would not know if she could practice in Germany. Worse yet, he did not know if she would be willing to go with him. Werner, once again pretending to have the power to read his thoughts, said:

"If she loves you, she will follow you to the end of the world. And if not, look for another that lives in Germany."

This was a situation that Oscar hoped he would not have to face.

"When do you want me to start?"

"January 2. You have the rest of November and December to leave your things in order in Johan. Patrick would not forgive me for stealing an employee, leaving him with unsolved problems."

"Patrick! I do not know how I'm going to tell him. He has been my mentor in this business."

"Just tell him you said yes. I talked to him before talking to you. He does not agree, but he knows that he cannot match my offer, and he thinks it would be unfair to hold you back."

That closed the deal, Oscar Brown would be, as of January of the year two thousand, the new President of Operations of Gewinn. How appropriate it would be to start the millennium with a new job.

CHAPTER FOUR

Paul Dieckens was in his home study in Washington. Sitting behind the majestic wooden desk, the current vice president of the United States was about to make the most important decision of his political career.

Accepting the nomination for the presidency of the country in the coming election would be the end point to his life as a public servant. If he lost the election, his career would end in a few months since no losing candidate would run again. It was as if they disappeared from the face of the earth. If he won, his career would extend to four or eight years. But it would always be the end. As a President, or as a losing candidate, he could no longer be eligible for any other public office. It was an important decision, perhaps the most important one in his life. (A candidate can run every four years, but a president can only serve 2 terms. No limit on the number of times a candidate can run, but they can only win election to two terms. They can run for other offices after those two terms, but not president or vice president.)

Paul held a glass of twelve-year-old scotch on ice in his hand. He usually drank domestic beer to support the industry, but for important decisions, scotch was always the spirit that helped him elucidate. With a drink in his right hand and an engagement ring in his left, he had decided to marry thirty years ago. Despite not remembering it, a drink was on the desk in his home in Minnesota when he made the decision to go into politics.

He had come to Minnesota in the 1960s, fleeing the New York hippies. It was love at first sight. He had arrived by car, and while driving without any particular destination, he was impressed by his surroundings. He had seen sceneries belonging to two seasons in less than a day. While crossing the state border between Iowa and Minnesota, one spring morning in April, he could see that the fields were being plowed and the landscape was blooming. Near two in the afternoon he arrived at the border with Canada, but he never crossed it. Suddenly, he was surrounded by snow as if it were the middle of winter. The young Paul Dieckens returned to the city of Minneapolis and settled there. A couple of years later he married a native of the state.

He felt comfortable in the state that was proclaimed cradle of inventions for adhesive tape, water skis, the stapler, and Spam. Golf could well be the official sport of Minnesota. Paul discovered it after a while and practiced it every time he found the opportunity.

Dieckens first came to public attention in 1975. Without any previous pretenses or previous experience in government, Paul launched himself with everything he had to win the elections for Governor of the State of Minnesota, remained in office for several consecutive periods. During the 80s he ran as a Congressman and won. After two more re-elections, he joined current President Dean Harding in his campaign formula. In the previous twenty-five years Paul had never lost an election, earning him the title of "Invincible Dieckens" in his party circle.

Anyone who knew him admired the warmth he instilled when shaking hands. His frank smile inspired confidence, despite his thin lips that were easily associated with severity of character. But what distinguished him most, what disarmed any woman, was the blue fire in his eyes.

With his mettle, he had defended and passed through Congress several laws and proposals that anyone else would have given up for lost causes. Not for Paul. When he proposed something, when he set a goal, he did not rest until he reached it.

Living the last eight years in Washington with free access to the White House had been an invaluable experience. His party wanted to remain in power, and he was a good prospect to continue occupying the Oval Office.

Paul sighed, emptying his mind of memories. It was the time to decide the future, and not to get lost in the past.

Would his streak of undefeated electoral winner continue in this new campaign? Would he achieve it? Was he ready for it? Those were his doubts. It was very easy to get carried away by the flattery of his party members. However, it would be his skin on fire and not theirs if he lost. He concluded that there was only one way to find out.

CHAPTER FIVE

Oscar Brown went to Patrick Johan's office on Friday to tender his resignation letter. As Werner had told him, there was neither surprise nor resentment.

"You leave a friend here. If you need me later, you know where to find me," were Johan's last words.

His recovery was almost complete. He no longer used crutches but continued with a cane to support his left leg as it was the most painful. Brown returned to his office without the heavy burden on his back, that of feeling like a traitor to Patrick's trust. He noted with satisfaction that the papers on his desk had reached their usual level. In two days, he had managed to catch up.

He sat down and did something he had almost never done before. In the bottom drawer he kept a bottle of whiskey and a couple of glasses. Oscar did not usually drink, but right now he needed something to motivate his senses. He took out the bottle and poured an inch, then called Linda on the intercom. When she arrived a few seconds later, the other glass was also served.

"What are we celebrating?"

"Linda, do not mention anything to anyone yet, but I'll only be here until the end of the year."

"I figured that. You're going to write to me from Germany, right?"

"Of course, yes. Take this. Sit down and then we'll get to work."

They both tossed back their drink in silence, and then Oscar returned the glasses and bottle to the drawer. They devoted themselves to their hard work as if nothing had happened.

* * *

During the week, Nora observed with pleasure how Oscar had recovered enough movement of his leg and arm.

She welcomed the weekend with joy, regardless of Friday night's madness at La Guardia airport. Oscar and Nora managed to get to Miami, that night, tired. They left the bags and went to bed. There was no romantic dinner. There were no kisses, no statements. However, they slept holding each other as they used to before his accident.

On Saturday morning, Nora woke up to find herself alone in bed. Oscar got up first and ordered breakfast delivered to the room. The immense terrace of the suite offered a view of the Atlantic.

Nora got up and when she left the room, she saw the waiter exit the room, closing the door behind him. Oscar stood at the terrace door and invited her to sit down and eat.

She enjoyed her second pancake when Oscar very quietly knelt by the table.

"Nora, would you marry me?"

Honest, short and straight to the heart. The most emotional things in life do not need many words when some gestures say it all.

Nora shed tears of emotion. He took out a black velvet box. When she opened it, Nora saw the most perfect engagement ring.

She took it delicately. The ring was white gold framing three diamonds: one large at the center with a smaller one on each side.

"It's beautiful!" She proclaimed.

Oscar smiled as she stood up. She took him by the hand as he stood. A mischievous smile crossed her lips as she guided him back to the room, skipping the rest of breakfast to concentrate on dessert.

They spent a passionate Saturday, choosing not to leave the suite. All the meals were from room service and served on the terrace.

Sunday found them in bed yet. Nora woke up feeling a tingling in her back. It was not the first time Oscar had done it. It was his subtle way of waking her up: touching her with the tip of his finger from the shoulders down the spine.

"Hmm. Good Morning!" She whispered as she stretched.

"Good morning, Nora. I have something important to tell you."

Nora turned to see Oscar, breathed easy seeing the serenity in the face of her future husband.

"Do you remember dinner on Thursday with the president of Gewinn?"

"Yes, but you never told me what he wanted."

"Well, he offered me a job," he said excitedly.

"Really? How wonderful! They are the biggest on the planet!" She said, then added, "What did they offer you?"

"President of Operations, and a compensation package that triples what I earn now."

Nora knew him very well. She knew from the look on his face he had not told her everything.

"The problem is that I have to live in Frankfurt, where the central offices are."

Nora understood what Oscar meant. She got up and walked around the room without noticing her nakedness while thinking. She struggled to analyze the situation with professional lucidity. If he left, she would have to follow him, but what about her career as a prosecutor? Her studies had been conducted in criminal, so she couldn't practice law in Germany. Maybe if she had studied international trade. It was too late for her to change course now.

"Oscar, I do not want to give up my career," she told him firmly, but the first tear betrayed her, rolling down her cheek before she finished.

"I know," he admitted. "But it's the best opportunity of my career. I can't waste it either."

Silence filled the room as their eyes met.

"Nora, please. I need you by my side."

"You don't think you can make it alone?" She said as she bit her lower lip without being able to control her weeping.

"No," he said, shaking his head.

Nora sighed. It was a difficult decision. On the one hand she did not want to lose the man she loved; on the other, she could not give up her career. She liked living in New York, being a prosecutor. At the same time, she understood Oscar's conflict: he could not give up the best opportunity of his career either. He was too good.

Nora lowered her head to study her hands carefully. The ring that she wore less than twenty-four had left no mark on her finger. She sat on the bed and took it off slowly, then handed it over.

Oscar received the ring and closed it in his fist, understanding the meaning. Nora watched the gesture of frustration.

"I think your sister was right. Our professions are our priority."

"Oscar ..." She closed her eyes and rested her head on his shoulder.

Nora got up after a minute and started dressing. They did not speak for the next hour while she packed and left the suite. He escorted her to the door, following her with his eyes down the hall. Nora's illusion to form a perfect marriage with Oscar Brown ended when the elevator doors closed.

Oscar walked back into the room. He couldn't contain himself anymore and threw himself on the bed. He buried his face in a pillow that silenced the cry of despair and frustration.

CHAPTER SIX

Frankfurt am Main, September 2000

The race for the presidency of the United States had begun. The primaries had already selected the two candidates, one for each party, who would compete for the White House. The governing party, which occupied the White House for eight years, wanted at least four more, nominating current Vice President Paul Dieckens. Everything was prepared for the great convention to be held in New York City in the first week of October. For its part, the opposition had nominated the Governor of the state of Florida, Robert Dolger. His acceptance speech included a string of criticism and accusations against the ruling party and was broadcast nationally during the convention of his party in the second week of September. This event was followed very closely by an American who lived in the city of Frankfurt am Main, Germany.

Oscar had presented himself to the embassy to ensure his participation by voting abroad.

Gewinn, the company he worked with, had reported above-average earnings for the last three quarterly closings. And although the media proposed the responsible person was the Executive

President, the German Werner Dietz, he proclaimed that much of the credit fell on the man he had just hired from Wall Street.

Oscar had come to Frankfurt sad from his emotional breakup. The sadness served as fuel to get more than ever buried at work, with a schedule of more than fourteen hours a day. He had also achieved total celibacy all that year. He had no time for romance. He took advantage of his weekends to see the different museums that abounded on the banks of the River Main. He also came to understand the fascination of Europeans with the opera when he visited the Opera House on a Saturday night.

At first, he had difficulty communicating, but in less than six months he spoke almost without an accent. His next goal was to learn to write German before the end of the year.

The offices of Gewinn are in the center of Frankfurt, one of the safest cities in Europe. Despite having the BMW of the year in the parking lot, Oscar preferred to walk the few blocks that separated his house from his office. It served as exercise and to clear his mind after a heavy day's work.

The evening of the last Friday of September found Oscar in his office, checking the closing of the stock exchange and closing week reports.

"Do you plan to go home at all?" Helga said before leaving.

His secretary, Helga Dystell, was an attractive woman who was hired because of her command of several European languages. At thirty, Helga spoke and wrote perfectly in English, German, French, and Italian, which are necessary for the performance of the work in the stock market.

"Yes, don't worry. I just want to finish seeing these reports."

"Mr. Brown, you can see those reports on your home computer. Remember that they are connected in a secure network."

Brown smiled at the reminder.

"The truth is that I prefer this view," he said as he pointed to the window next to him.

Helga observed for a moment through the window. It provided a spectacular view of the city, but she sensed that her boss's reasons were different.

"Very well. See you on Monday."

"Auf wiedersehen!"

The secretary left. Once again, Oscar was left alone in his office. Every time his subconscious reminded him of Nora: some woman with a similar hairstyle, a fragrance, some of the many movies they had seen together, on her birthday, any of the thousands of details that make up a relationship of more than two years, he clung to his work.

While talking with Helga, the screensaver activated on his computer. He stopped for a moment to admire the emblem. The Gewinn logo was a red rectangle from which three bars were pointing steeply to the left. The upper one was a little longer than the second and the other little more than the last one. In the center of the rectangle was a white circle enclosing a solitary "G" in a black bold font. Under the circle was the name of the company also in black letters: Gewinn

Oscar had the impression of looking at inverted stairs. But most people associated it with a hand with outstretched fingers that were about to grab something or the tips of an eagle's feathers. He supposed that the first association was due to the extensive business and influences that the company had. The second left it alone in the plane of his subconscious. Over the years, several firms had tried to sabotage it, resorting to various methods ranging from smear campaigns to demands for monopolistic practices, but Gewinn always came out well.

For several minutes, Oscar contemplated the emblem. In the end, he reacted, moved the mouse and Gewinn's hand that had him captivated vanished. In its place appeared a spreadsheet with several columns of names and numbers. The executive sighed and studied the report.

A few hours later, he left his office and walked, as was his custom, to his house. After a few blocks, a man with a cigarette in his mouth approached him.

"Hast du Feuer?" the man asked.

Not having the habit of smoking, Oscar shook his head. Another guy approached from behind and he felt something sharp against his back. He stiffened; it was the first time he had been assaulted.

"Don't move," the man said.

What caught Oscar's attention was that he spoke to him in English and not German. At that moment, a car pulled up and the back door opened. The three men walked towards the vehicle. The captive offered no resistance. Once inside, he could see the driver and another man in the passenger seat, then a hard blow to the base of the neck left him unconscious.

* * *

He awoke with a start because of the water that had been thrown in his face. He noticed that his feet were tied to the legs of the chair with a thick gray ribbon, and he felt a twinge in his shoulders when he realized that his hands were also tied behind his back. It was an awkward position that made it difficult to breathe. When he managed to focus his eyesight, he could see the man who had asked for a light in front of him.

He exceeded two meters in height, athletic body and black hair. His complexion was white, but the most striking feature of his face was his green eyes, around which one could see the marks left by the passage of time. Oscar estimated his age to be about fifty years, maybe more. He wore dark blue jeans and a black leather jacket, white collar shirt with the top button open and in his right hand, he held a glass.

"Who are you?" Oscar asked.

"My name is Adolf Hoffman, Mr. Brown. But I think it will be more important to know who you are."

Oscar had no idea what the man was talking about. Looking around, he noticed he was in a small room. To his right was a circular table and another chair, in front of him was a double bed, while the walls shouted the coldness and lack of personality that only a seedy hotel of death can offer.

"I do not know what you're talking about."

"I'm talking about your past, Mr. Brown, your father and your grandfather." His voice was serious. He spoke slowly but well-articulated. "Do you have any idea who they were?"

Talking about his father always brought Oscar unpleasant memories. He never talked about this with anyone. But now this stranger asked him about his father.

With certain serenity in his voice, he replied, "My father died when I was six years old, I never met my grandfather."

"I know all that, Mr. Brown. I witnessed the accident in which your father died. We better talk about your grandfather, which is the main reason for this meeting."

"I don't know anything about my grandfather. I never met him. My father was an illegitimate child. That's why I only carry my grandmother's last name."

Hoffman sat on the edge of the bed, facing Oscar, their faces a few centimeters apart

"I met your grandfather. My father was his doctor. He diagnosed your grandmother's pregnancy, and that's why he was murdered."

His gaze showed the vehemence of what he was saying, but Oscar could not understand why this man had bound him. Almost in a deranged monologue, Adolf continued.

"It was necessary that the pregnancy was kept a secret so that the plan of Helmut Dietz worked." He smiled in a sardonic way and said, "Helmut is the father of your boss, Werner."

Adolf got up and started pacing around the room. "But I think I'm confusing you. Let me tell you everything from the beginning."

* * *

In 1945 I was thirteen years old and I was enrolled in the Hitler's Youth. They hadn't sent me to the front only because my father was the Führer's favorite doctor. They were friends since the beginning of the Nazi movement. That's why my father baptized me with his name. My duties in those days were to take care of the refuge where families of influence hid. My beloved Berlin was in ruins, and I was annoyed because I was watching the end of the war and witnessing Germany as the loser. Already the Russians were about to enter the city. Every day we could listen to the cannons coming closer. In the afternoons, I walked to the bunker where my father took care of Hitler and we returned together. I was his escort. My mother and my younger brother had died in a bombing, so we only had each other. We became best friends.

One day at the end of April, as I approached the shelter, I managed to hear my father's voice telling someone that he'd forgive him. That he understood

that he was carrying out orders. Upon hearing this, my little military training told me not to hurry. I threw myself on the ground and crawled to the corner of the building. From there, I got to see an SS soldier who was pointing a submachine gun at my father. My father was facing me, but the soldier was facing away. However, I heard his apologies. Apparently, my father had cured him of some illness sometime before and the soldier was grateful, but he had orders to execute him.

At that moment, I took out the knife that was in my belt. I was able to get on my knees in the corner, and like a cat, I jumped on that soldier's back. I caught him off guard and managed to cut his throat with my knife, but his finger was already on the trigger and he fired. The shots hit my father.

The soldier and I fell to the ground. I ran to my father. His uniform was stained with blood. A row of holes ran from his stomach to his right shoulder. I understood that he did not have much time to live.

With his left hand, my father took out a small diary that he had in his pocket and handed it to me. Finally, he told me he was proud of me and then he died.

Watching my father die in my arms was a terrifying experience. After all, I was only thirteen years old. I did not understand why they wanted to kill him, but I thought the diary would explain it to me.

A few minutes later I ran. I ran until I could not. When I stopped, I saw that I was out of town. It was getting dark and there was a ceasefire. That night I slept in the field. When I woke up, I ripped off all the insignia from my uniform and kept running.

When I passed by a road, I saw a vehicle without marks or plates. I thought I saw Fräulein Braun in it. I had known her for a while. Shortly after, I ran into a patrol of Soviet soldiers while they ate. They, seeing my dirty and shabby uniform, thought I was some deserter. I had not eaten for more than twenty-four hours and the soldiers shared their rations.

That day I had the opportunity to read my father's diary. He wrote about the gloomy atmosphere in the bunker, but almost at the end he made a note about having checked Fräulein Braun and determining that she was pregnant.

Over time, knowing that according to official version Eva Braun and Hitler himself had committed suicide in the bunker, before the Russians arrived, I understood the basics of the plan, since I had seen her escape from that place.

When his captor finished the story, Oscar understood that he identified Oscar as Adolf Hitler's grandson. But that couldn't be true. It is true that his last name looked like the Americanized version of Braun, but ... that was a crazy story.

"Do you not believe me yet?" Hoffman asked.

"No, I don't," Oscar told him with all the conviction he could muster.

"What's your father's name?"

"Dennis."

"Dennis, right. And you are Oscar. I guess that was part of the original plan. Dennis begins with the second letter of the name Adolf. The possible meaning is that he was the second. Your name begins with the third letter of the name Adolf. The letter O. Can you not see the pattern?"

This argument had coherence, but Oscar wished he could dismiss it as a simple coincidence. Common sense told him it could be true, but he refused to admit it.

"I don't believe you. In fact, I think you're crazy," he told Hoffman.

The man was enraged. He shouted and threw the glass against the wall. It exploded into pieces.

"Well, you'd better believe it, because it's the damn truth!"

One of the splinters hit Oscar on the cheek. He felt a drop of blood sliding down his chin.

Adolf saw it with disgust and commented, "That's the blood of the greatest murderer of the twentieth century. I'll leave you for a while to think about what I just said."

As Hoffman left the room, Oscar saw two other men outside the doorway, watching.

Oscar sighed. He could not believe what he had just heard. However, one thing he did understand was that his captor believed it with vehemence. His final comment about the blood was proof of his conviction.

He turned his head to either side, looking around the room, looking for something, some explanation, some hope of what to do. He lowered his gaze and, less than a meter away, at the foot of his chair was another shard with a sharp point. As a revelation, Oscar began to sway and fell sideways. The carpet cushioned the blow. He crawled until the piece was within reach of one of his bound hands. Holding the glass fragment, he cut one of his fingers. He cursed, but he continued with his plan. He grabbed the object that symbolized his hope and began to cut through his bonds.

It was difficult at first, but he succeeded after a few minutes. With his hands now free, he got a better grip of the piece of glass and cut the ties on his feet. In less than a minute he sat up, dropped the glass.

The blood from his middle finger covered his right hand. He squeezed it with his thumb. He went stealthily and hurriedly to the window. As he went out to the balcony, he was able to determine his location. He was at a small hotel located a few blocks from his office. He had walked several times on that street when he walked Helga home on the days when they worked late. Helga's house was closer than his own, so he decided to go there. Adjoining the balcony, were the emergency stairs. He hurriedly descended them. When he reached the street, he walked hurriedly, accelerating more and more as he turned the corner and then ran wildly.

He arrived at the building where his secretary lived. He pressed the intercom button. Nothing happened. Oscar repeated the action and waited a few seconds. Desperate, he left his finger pressing the button until he heard the familiar voice over the intercom.

"Yes?"

"Helga, thank God! It's Oscar. I need to talk to you. Open, please," he pleaded.

Immediately he heard the dry sound of the electric door, pushed it and rushed in. He ran up the stairs and when he got to Helga's apartment, she met him at the door.

When she saw him, she was alarmed by the dry blood and the look of anguish on her boss' face. She invited him in and sat him in the living room. Then she went to the kitchen and returned with a bowl of water and a rag. She sat in front of Oscar and began to clean his face.

"You know, Mr. Brown, this was not in my job description." She smiled, then added, "What happened? Did they rob you?

Oscar grimaced, remembering that all this had begun under the impression of a robbery. At that moment he wished it had been just that.

"In a matter of speaking, Helga. What they really stole was my past."

CHAPTER SEVEN

Dean Harding, as President of the United States, was not required to work on a Saturday morning. He usually spent the weekend with his children and wife, trying to spend as much time as possible with them.

The part of the White House where the First Family resided had a studio and an informal room for work meetings.

That particular Saturday, it had as a guest Paul Dieckens, the vice president. The two men spoke of the points to be discussed at the next party convention in which Paul would be officially nominated for the presidential candidacy.

They sat on the comfortable sofa. The coffee table held sandwiches that the men wolfed down while savoring their favorite brand of beer. Dean preferred Heineken, while Paul, supporting the domestic market, took a Miller.

"So, do you think I should avoid the issue of abortion?"

"Of course. The country is divided on this issue. So, no matter what you answer, you'll always have someone against you," Dean replied.

"Perfect. But I think that sooner or later some journalist will ask."

"Yes, but better leave it for later in the campaign."

At that moment the telephone rang, only five people in the world had that number. President Harding got up and walked to the desk to answer. He listened for a few seconds and gave his consent for something that Paul could not hear. He hung up the phone and sat down again as he explained to his friend what was happening.

"Chuck and Andy are here. It seems that there is a situation in Europe that I should know about." Charles "Chuck" Mayer was the Chief of Staff at the White House and Andy Pearson was the Chief of National Security. Dean and Paul were sure it must be important if both men came to the residence on a Saturday morning.

"Should I leave?"

"You better stay. Sooner or later you will find out. Also, as an official candidate, you have the right to be informed of my decisions. It's only going to be a minute and then we can continue with the campaign."

A few minutes later the new guests arrived. The President received them very courteously and prepared drinks for them. After eight years, Dean knew the drinks of each of the men who worked near him. The fact of serving them in this way, being the highest ranked, relaxed them a little and it was with those little gestures that Harding got the men to swear loyalty and notify him of any problem in time to resolve it and not when it was too late.

"What's wrong, Chuck?" he asked at once, serving him whiskey with soda.

"A few minutes ago, we received a report from Israel," Andy responded as it was his work area involved.

"What's going on?"

"It seems that they have just discovered one more tentacle of their eternal enemy. Through the Mossad, their secret service, they discovered the reason why Hitler married Eva Braun before committing suicide. She was pregnant." Pearson allowed a few moments for the group to process the information.

"But what does that imply? She also committed suicide, right?" Paul asked.

"Apparently not. She was smuggled to the United States where she had her son. The woman they burned in the bunker in Berlin was a double," Andy explained.

"You must be kidding," said the President, who could not believe that he spent time on this on a Saturday morning.

"I hope so. But they say they have evidence. Apparently, it was a last-minute plan that a certain Helmut Dietz devised," Andy continued.

"Wait. That name is familiar to me," Paul said.

"Of course, he's the father of Werner Dietz."

"Are you telling me that one of the twenty richest men in the world is the son of a Nazi?" Harding asked.

"That's not all. Dietz has plans that include the descendant of Hitler. Eva's son, who Americanized her surname to Brown, died in 1976. But in the seventies, he had married and had a son, Oscar Brown, the current president of Gewinn operations," said the Head of National Security, and then continued, "I think Israel wants to eliminate the problem at the root by removing Werner Dietz and Oscar Brown."

"This is the first time that Israel has asked for permission to carry out their executions. I still remember the Olympic Games of '72," Harding said.

"They are not asking for permission. In fact, they only let filter what we just told you, because of the agreement we have to share information. They did not even classify it as urgent. They only transmitted it among a thousand other data files," Chuck explained.

"Why, do you think they are plotting something?" the vice president asked.

"Because of the way they show the information. They try to distract us, to make us believe that they do not intend to do anything. Then, when they execute their plan, we cannot plead ignorance. They do it this way so we do not get offended when it appears in the newspaper that an American was murdered abroad."

"Good heavens!" Harding exclaimed.

* * *

Jacob Goldberg, in his capacity as the director of the Mossad, was considered the most powerful man in Israel, after the Prime Minister. Goldberg was a survivor of Auschwitz. When he turned eighteen, he did not hesitate to enlist in the army, where he had an enviable career. After six months he was assigned to secret operations and, little by little, he climbed up to reach the highest place of the little known, but terribly efficient, Mossad.

In the spy community, Goldberg built his reputation through his unusual methods, cunning and, most of all, courage. Since the death of his wife five years before, it wasn't strange for Goldberg to spend a weekend in his office on the top floor of a residential area of Tel Aviv.

Goldberg was reading the execution order against Oscar Brown, which was already signed by the Prime Minister of Israel. This had been the last addition to the permanent list maintained by the Mossad. The list was composed of Israel's enemies. In the beginning, they were mostly Nazis, but over time they had been replaced by terrorists or any other individual or group that was considered a threat to the State. The current Prime Minister had approved the list, which is kept in his safe and a copy in the Mossad Director's office. The first had insisted on an express request before each execution. This was processed by Goldberg and now he was plotting at his desk.

His assistant entered the windowless office that was checked every Monday morning for the presence of microphones or other surveillance devices.

"What happened?" he asked.

"We just received confirmation that the CIA already has all the information on Gewinn."

"All right. Then we can proceed."

The young man nodded but did not move, opened his mouth to say something but held back before speaking. Goldberg didn't take his eyes off him and smiled benevolently.

"You have worked with me for five years and still do not dare to say what you think."

"I do not think it's appropriate, sir. I'm just an assistant."

"I know something is bothering you. Speak."

"I don't think the Americans are in total agreement. After all, it is a US citizen that we are going to eliminate."

"That doesn't matter. We were not asking for permission. We send them the information only as a professional courtesy. Gewinn is a potential threat not only to Israel, but to the entire world. Washington should see it that way, too, and I bet they're grateful that we'll do the dirty work this time, even if their pride does not allow them to admit it."

The assistant nodded and left the office. Goldberg leaned back in his huge executive chair and turned toward the wall that showed a huge map of Israel and neighboring countries. His gaze fell on a framed photo showing the ruins of a Nazi concentration camp. In a corner of the image, the flag of the Reich was evident as it was burned by several men. At once he sighed contentedly.

"Maybe now we can free ourselves forever from you, and from your entire lineage."

CHAPTER EIGHT

Oscar spent the weekend in Helga's apartment. She treated him as the best of guests, although he always slept on the sofa. Helga only left once on Saturday to the supermarket to buy food.

Oscar told her the full story that Hoffman had told him. She was incredulous. Oscar entertained the option of reporting Hoffman to the police. What information could he provide them?

Most likely, after finding that Brown had escaped, they would have left the hotel.

"I'm still unconvinced that the idea was to kill you."

"Why do you say that?"

"Because killing you would have been easier on the street where they caught you. I believe they had other plans for you."

"What other plans could they possibly have for me?" Oscar asked surprised.

"I'm not sure. Maybe money."

"It would be something very elaborate to be a kidnapping and ransom."

"Perhaps. Yet, people don't usually take future murder victims to hotels."

Helga was silent while thinking. Oscar noticed that his secretary's hair was not all black. A few strokes of brown could be seen at the root. Her round face with honey eyes was complemented with perfect lips. Helga bit her lower lip as she always did when she thought intensely about something. It was a habit that her boss had observed before.

"Maybe they were planning to kill you and make it look like an accident. I don't know, some overdose of drugs and abandon you at the hotel."

Oscar paled at that idea. He spent Sunday thinking what he could do, what his options were. In the end, he decided it was best to talk to Werner Dietz.

On Monday at seven thirty in the morning, Oscar left the apartment with Helga. She had been wearing the same outfit since Friday although she had washed it over the weekend. They caught a taxi to the offices of Gewinn. Oscar hastened to take the elevator to the ninth floor. Upon arrival, he met Olga in the anteroom of Werner's office. The assistant greeted him politely and then told him Werner would receive him immediately.

Genuine works of art adorned the walls. At the back, a sliding glass door opened onto a terrace where Mr. Dietz received important customers. On the wall behind his desk was a world map, in which were pins with red dots, the offices of Gewinn throughout the world. The map had been specially printed for the company and had the red, black and white logo in the lower right corner.

Brown looked at everything with different eyes that day and felt himself a prisoner of those walls.

"My dear Oscar, what are you doing here so early?" Werner asked. He was sitting in his chair as he gestured for Oscar to sit in front of him.

Oscar took his time relating the story of what happened over the weekend. Dietz watched him without missing a detail, but his face didn't show any reaction, surprise or amazement. Nothing at all. At the end of the narrative, Werner just leaned back in his chair and smiled.

"It was time you knew, but I would have preferred to tell you. You can be sure I would not have tied you up to tell you, though," Werner said.

This was the final blow for Oscar, the loss of his hopes that Hoffman was a madman. He stood and walked to the window.

"How?" He asked after a few seconds that seemed to stretch to eternity.

"My father came up with this plan on the same day that Fräulein Braun's pregnancy was confirmed. He was in the bunker with the Führer. They got the double that looked like her, and they made her take the cyanide pills. Then Hitler committed suicide and both bodies were burned, as the story says."

"But what was the original plan? I don't get it."

"The plan was for Hitler's son, your father, to take possession of the fortune that had been hidden for him. And with that, to re-form the Nazi party, take Germany back and continue with the work."

"You guys approached my father?"

"Yes, in 1976. He refused. That's why he died."

Oscar clenched his fist. He wondered, at that moment, if he would share his father's fate should he not to accede to Werner's request.

"The times have changed Oscar. We no longer need that mass leader of the twentieth century. Now everything moves for money. When your father refused, we understood this and we took actions to ensure the future of our ideals, but on another level. Look at that map on the wall. I got what your grandfather never did. I dominate Moscow. Gewinn has offices in countries that belonged to the Third Reich, and even those that he could never conquer, such as the Soviet Union and the United States. The legacy of your grandfather no longer exists. The Aryan supremacy will be demonstrated in another way, without the need for so many deaths."

Werner confirmed the crazy story that Oscar had refused to believe. The fact that they no longer needed Oscar set off warning bells in his mind. This was too much for anyone, even Oscar, who began to breathe hard. He felt a heaviness in his chest and felt the panic of a man who believed he was about to suffer cardiac arrest.

"Then, why do you need me now?" He asked, afraid to hear the answer.

"We have plans for you."

"What if I refuse?"

"We hope you have better judgment than your father."

Both men stared into each other's eyes. Werner showing the same smile with which he convinced Oscar to join Gewinn the year before.

"Still not convinced? Do you want a true show of power?"

"What are you going to do?"

"You'll see. Tell me, what is the second largest bank in Switzerland?"

"Bank Suisse Corporation. Why?"

"You'll see." Dietz took the phone and dialed. A few seconds passed. "Franz? Hi, I need you to do something. Apply the treatment to the Bank Suisse Corporation." He waited a few seconds in silence and then said, "Yes, that same one. Goodbye."

He hung up and as a man who knows himself master of the situation, told Oscar "I suggest you search the newspapers well on Wednesday. Although I would be surprised if it does not come out on the front pages."

At that moment, Helga entered accompanied by someone unknown to Oscar. She looked different in some way, walked with more poise. Her gaze was fixed on Werner. She stopped three paces from the desk, raising her right hand. Until that moment, Oscar had not seen the weapon.

With the greatest peace of mind, Helga Dystell fired three shots into the chest of Werner, who fell at his desk. Oscar, surprised, turned to Helga who held his gaze firmly.

Without noticing Oscar, the other man also raised his right hand and fired only once. This was not a conventional weapon, but an air pistol.

Oscar felt a sting in the neck and clutched the site of the pain. He felt something like a needle, removed it from his neck to look at it. It was a metallic dart, from the tip dripped a whitish solution. Two seconds later, his world went dark.

CHAPTER NINE

Oscar woke up tied again. The drug they had used to drop him was very powerful. His head seemed to burst with pain. It was worse than the day after a drunken stupor.

When he opened his eyes, he saw the ceiling. He was tied up on a bed. Each of his four extremities was tied separately to each corner, his body forming a cross. Whoever had done it was a professional. When he raised his head, he could feel that he had several pillows under him. To his right was a window with the curtains closed. Reproductions of famous paintings like Mona Lisa and others hung on the walls.

There were two doors in front, one an exit and the other, possibly, the bathroom. To his left, there was a piece of wood and next to it a large mirror behind a table where he saw makeup jars, brushes, and hairspray, among other feminine products. On the left side of the headboard, Helga sat in backward chair with her hands resting on the backrest.

"Good morning," she said.

"What's going on?" he asked in the midst of the pain.

"I'm really sorry, Oscar."

"What are you sorry for? Betraying my trust or tying me to a bed?" Oscar was afraid to hear the answer.

"I work for the intelligence service of Israel. I was assigned as your secretary to watch over you."

"I suppose your name is not Helga Dystell, then."

"It's not, But I can´t tell you my real name anyway."

"What are you going to do with me?"

"It will not be long before the news that Werner Dietz was murdered in his office, and that everything seems to indicate that you were the guilty party will be out."

"Perfect!" Oscar said, "first they accuse me of being Hitler's grandson, and now they are going to accuse me of a murder I didn't commit."

"We were suspicious of Werner some time ago, but we had not been able to infiltrate until the opportunity of a secretary for you was presented. Dietz did not want to use anyone from the company, but he did outsource," she explained.

"What a miracle you didn't try to seduce him," Oscar said sarcastically.

Helga smiled before answering. "We tried, but Werner was homosexual. Did you know?"

"No," Oscar admitted.

"Once you are wanted as Dietz's killer, you will appear dead somewhere in the city."

"The police are going to investigate. They are not so gullible."

"Of course, they aren't. But your suicide note will explain everything. Your relationship with that genocide, and what Werner had proposed to you. In the end, you will be a hero for not wanting to follow in the footsteps of your family."

Oscar's mind travelled to the past, trying to figure out how he had come to this situation. He finally arrived at the hotel room where he proposed to Nora Miller. At that moment he concluded that his first mistake was not to stay in the United States with her.

"Helga, you're judging me for something I was not party to. It doesn't matter who my grandfather is. I'm not even sure about that. But you have worked with me in recent months, and you know me. You know that I am incapable of murder."

Dystell interrupted him by rising suddenly. "I'm sorry," she said and went out of the room.

"Yes, you already said that," he said cynically.

Helga stopped for a second. It even seemed like she was going to turn back. But in the end, she straightened her back and left the room.

* * *

"... and now we go to the chief of police for a statement."

The television image changed from the news anchor to the image of a man standing in front of huge glass doors with the Gewinn logo in the center.

"This is a very peculiar case. Not only was Mr. Werner killed, but also his secretary," said the man appeared to be a policeman.

The journalist withdrew the microphone from the interviewee and held it close. "Any suspects so far?"

"It's too early to make any judgement. At the moment we are interviewing all possible witnesses, but I can´t comment on an investigation in progress," concluded the man who immediately started walking away, leaving the journalists throwing questions into the air.

The image returned to the news anchor in the studio.

"Up to this moment, the police have not given any other statement. However, an unofficial source confirmed that the last employee to enter the office was the current President of Operations, the American, Oscar Brown. We tried to locate him, without success, for an interview. And with this, we turn to the weather report ..."

Hoffman turned off the television with the remote control. He remained thoughtful. He had followed and studied Oscar Brown for more than three years. There was even a time when he thought he was wrong. His doubts were alleviated when he learned that Werner Dietz traveled to the United States to hire him.

He couldn't believe that Oscar was capable of committing a cold-blooded murder, especially after knowing the truth. Murdering a person is not easy, he thought. He had started at thirteen, but his story was different. Brown had not grown up in a war environment, had not heard bombings at night and cannons during the day.

Something was not right. One of his favorite hobbies was putting together puzzles, the more pieces the better. Now what he had heard on the news was certainly a puzzle, but he knew there were certain pieces missing.

* * *

By Tuesday morning, the news had already gone around the world. Andy Pearson was in his small office in the White House, analyzing several security reports, although this news had been heard on television. In his mind he was reviewing Saturday's meeting at President Harding's residence. It was amazing how quickly Israel's service could work. They had the reputation of being a very efficient team. In Pearson's eyes, they just proved it once again.

* * *

Of the people who heard the news, no one was more surprised than the prosecutor Nora Miller. She never would have thought about Oscar as a killer, because he had always been a hopeless romantic around her. The reputation of a strong and unscrupulous man in the offices of Johan Trading vanished in bed when he was with her.

What could have brought Oscar to the point of murder? Nora did not understand, but she tried to, with all her strength.

CHAPTER TEN

"Who's the man that accompanies you? The one who shot me," Oscar asked his kidnapper.

Helga was sitting by the bed, feeding him. He remained tied except to go to the bathroom. In that case, Helga's companion went in with him. He was never out of their sight.

"I can't tell you."

"Oh please! I'm going to pay for your crime. I have the right to know."

Helga considered this for a few seconds, and finally said, "His papers say his name is Hans."

"That's more common than Smith in the United States," Oscar said as he chewed on the bite of sandwich in his mouth.

Dystell smiled and said, "That's the idea."

The diet of the last few hours had consisted exclusively of sandwiches in whole wheat bread and water. Oscar had an athletic body, always careful of his diet. Being subjected to this type of diet wasn't difficult. Especially when he knew that his last meal would be one of these sandwiches. Helga had already revealed the whole plan.

The woman held a glass with a long straw so that Oscar could drink. He emptied the glass.

"Alright. I think we're finished here." She got up and headed for the door.

"Helga, wait."

She stopped and turned to face Oscar. He watched her closely. She was now dressed in casual clothes, black jeans and a baggy red blouse. Quite different from the tailored suits he used to see her in at work. The new wardrobe made her look younger.

"Helga, please, don't do this to me. I want to live. I am not to blame for what many people I never knew did."

"I told you before. The injuries that Adolf Hitler did to the people of Israel are very deep, no matter how many years have passed. We cannot forget the six million of the Holocaust."

With that said, she left the room and closed the door. He had managed to see the dark sky through a window when Helga went out.

Despite being in bed, the position in which he was tied was uncomfortable, and he was tired. Finally, the tiredness overcame the worries and he closed his eyes.

A sudden noise woke him. He raised his head and saw a black figure coming through the window.

The man walked towards the bed. He was wearing a mask, and only deep green eyes were distinguishable. Oscar thought he recognized them. The man was staring at him, then his gaze fell on the ropes that pinned Oscar to the bed.

The man raised his right hand, and Oscar could see a gun with a very long barrel, a silencer. He walked toward the door of the room, turned the latch very carefully and opened it a few centimeters, aiming the gun through the opening. Oscar noticed a small flash and the movement of the man's arm, but his ears did not register the solitary shot.

Then the man left the room. It was silent as a tomb. Oscar didn't know what to think about this new turn of events. It surely wasn't part of his secretary's plan either. Suddenly, he heard something, a strong blow. It was followed by the indisputable sound of glass breaking. He deduced that it was a fight. By the noises he heard, it didn't last long.

A few seconds later the door burst open, but instead of the masked one that Oscar hoped to see, it was Helga.

She went to the bed, a knife in her hand. She crouched beside the bed and began to cut the bonds that held Oscar's hands. She had a cut eyelid and a busted lower lip. While cutting the ropes, Oscar noticed she was spitting blood on the bed. Dystell cut the straps off his legs and sat on the bed to take a breath.

Oscar managed to get up. His back screamed in pain from having been in the same position for so long, but now wasn't the time to complain. Helga went to the window and beckoned him out first. Oscar reached it, and poked his head out. There was a balcony outside, like the hotel where he had escaped from Hoffman. In that instant, he recognized the green eyes behind the mask, and he understood what had happened. Helga wasn't saving his life. She was protecting her plan. Oscar's death had to close the case of Werner Dietz. If they found him tied to a bed, it would be difficult to prove a suicide case, no matter what the note said.

Once on the balcony, he watched as Helga came out after him. They started down the stairs to the first level. In the alley, Helga walked close behind him but collapsed. Oscar tried to catch her but the two fell to the ground.

Oscar removed a bag hanging from her shoulder and examined her. She had a deep wound in her side. His knowledge of wounds wasn't extensive, but he determined it must have been a knife.

She had a pulse, although very weak. However, she was heavily bleeding. Oscar took her in his arms, carried her out of the alley and flagged down a taxi. The driver hurried to help with the wounded young woman.

"I think someone assaulted her. I found her lying around the corner," Oscar lied.

He still wore his suit shirt and pants. Fortunately, the taxi driver did not notice he was barefoot. Between the two they placed her into the back seat of the vehicle. Oscar put his hand into his pocket and found the money he always carried for unexpected expenses. He pulled out a few bills and gave them to the taxi driver.

"Take her to the nearest hospital."

"How about you?" the driver asked.

"I don't know her, but I couldn't leave her lying in the street either. Take her to the hospital, please. Say you found her. I can't get too involved." The driver didn't look convinced, so Oscar added, "You have no idea how jealous my wife is."

"Oh, I see," the man cracked a smile that spoke of a shared curse with their spouses.

Convinced of the lies, the taxi driver got into the car and drove off in the direction of the hospital.

Oscar stood on the sidewalk, watching the taxi drive away, admiring the ease with which he had lied to the stranger. It was a convincing, realistic lie that explained the situation very well, and Oscar had devised it in the heat of the moment. After a minute, Oscar turned around and headed for the alley to look for Helga's purse.

* * *

All the cities of the world, no matter how big or how small they are, always have an area that they recommend the tourist not to approach. Frankfurt am Main was no different from other cities, and it was precisely in this dangerous area where the desperate apparent grandson of Adolf Hitler had managed to hide from those who persecuted him.

A few blocks away he rented a room in a rundown hotel. It was already Wednesday, and he had no idea what to do or where to go. Oscar was sitting in front of the television watching the news of the day. The news of the death of the president of Gewinn had appeared in the headlines. To this was added the more recent news that had scared the financial world: the bankruptcy of the Bank Suisse Corporation.

Oscar gasped in surprise. The old bastard kept his promise. In just two working days, a bank more than a hundred years old, the second in its country, and fifth in Europe, went bankrupt.

He supposed that Werner had chosen that bank for some special reason, not by chance. The fact that the bank was in Switzerland meant it must have been on purpose. The same Switzerland that remained outside the Second World War to declare itself a neutral country since the beginning of the conflict.

The last news comment indicated that Oscar Brown was wanted by the police, especially since he had disappeared. In addition, as the end of the report said they had tried to interview Brown's mother, who lived in Paris, but she had suffered cardiac arrest and was currently in critical condition.

This news worried Oscar. What could he do now? He felt as if his head was about to explode. In search of a glimmer of hope, he emptied the contents of Helga's bag on the bed. There were four passports: two with different names and nationalities and two others for who he supposed was her partner. In addition, there was enough cash, perhaps enough for a hasty escape, a couple of keys, two cell phones, a Swiss army knife, and four credit cards, one for each passport.

He took a passport and reviewed the description and the photo carefully.

This gave him an idea. He returned everything to the bag, took some money and left the room in a hurry.

Two hours later, the man who looked in the mirror was very similar to the one in the photo. Oscar had not shaved since Friday morning, and now he had a beard and mustache a little shorter than the one in the photo. He applied bleach he had bought, and the color was almost identical.

On Thursday, very early, he left the hotel and went to the train station on Meinheimer Street. When he crossed the bridge over the Main, he thought maybe it would be the last time he would be in Frankfurt. In the past year he had learned to love that city, its museums, its streets, its rhythm of life.

But now everything was different, Oscar was in the middle of a crisis that had begun less than a week before.

The station was in the eastern part of the city. When Oscar arrived, he saw more police than usual. He had already taken trains earlier to go to Berlin. He liked to travel that way. It reminded him of earlier times, that he had lived vicariously through the movies. He found it curious that the bad guy always tried to escape by train, and this was now his escape route, at the beginning of the twenty-first century!

He bought a ticket to Paris with cash. The train left at 8:45 in the morning. Meanwhile, he went to a kiosk, bought a couple of newspapers and a coffee. Then he looked for a bench to wait for his departure.

CHAPTER ELEVEN

No one can think of Paris, the city of light, without associating it with the Eiffel Tower, the Notre Dame Cathedral, or the Arc de Triomphe. Nobody can resist the inherent romance professed by the city, immortalized by the pen of Victor Hugo and Alexandre Dumas.

Oscar's visit was far from those pleasures. In what he now considered his previous life, as President of Operations for Gewinn, he visited the city often because his mother resided there. And now she was again the reason for which he had undertaken this trip. He knew he was wanted by the German police and that Interpol would probably have been alerted. Oscar was traveling under the name of Günther König, using one of the passports he had found in Helga's purse.

While doing his customs process, he could see on one of the televisions that a picture of him was being shown. The volume was muted, so he heard nothing of what they said about him. The woman who checked his passport looked at the screen for a fraction of a second, then the passport photo. She reached for a list that was at her side and scanned it quickly, looking for the name König. He held his breath, expecting the worst. In the end, satisfied with her rigorous inquiries, she stamped Günther's passport and returned it, wishing him a pleasant stay in Paris. Oscar thanked her in French laced with a heavy German accent and moved on.

When leaving the train station, he crossed the street and went to a bank where he changed Dutch Marks into Francs. In his previous trips, Oscar had learned that the French people are much kinder if one used their currency and tried to use their language. There is obvious contempt for foreign currencies and languages. The new plan to establish the Euro as the single currency of Europe was still in the process of being implemented, but Oscar knew that this would be a blow to French pride.

He caught a taxi and asked to be taken to a hospital a few blocks away from his mother's apartment. During the train trip he had concluded that if she was hospitalized, it should be in this hospital.

His fugitive situation had also taught him to be careful. Knowing that there was a florist across the street from that hospital he went there first. He paid a large amount in cash and signed the card as André, as his mother's neighbor was called. The next step was easy. He went to the hospital corridor and sat down to wait. It was a large medical center, so his presence went unnoticed. He waited and every time he saw a boy come in to deliver flowers, he would move close to hear the name. It was the third time before he heard that they were asking for Carolyn Brown's room.

He followed the nurse who took the flowers. She climbed the stairs, then turned to the right, walked down a long white corridor that smelled of disinfectant and cleaners. The nurse entered a room on the left, room 521.

Oscar, stealthily walked past the door. At the end of the hall there was a small waiting room. He sat down, waiting until the nurse came out before he slipped into the room.

His mother slept. Her emaciated face showed how much weight she had lost. He recalled that his last visit had been almost two months before. The bouquet he had ordered was placed between two others. He read the cards. One was from the real André, which he found funny. He took the card he had signed. The sender of the other arrangement was Nora, his ex-fiancée. He hadn't seen that coming.

He sat on the bed and stroked his mother's face. She woke up when she felt the human touch and appeared excited to see him. Regardless of the beard, the bleach or any other disguise, his mother recognized Oscar at once. He put his finger to his mouth indicating silence. She calmed down and waited for him to speak.

"Hello, Mother."

"Oh, Oscar. I knew you'd come," she said is a near-whisper. She gazed at him with all the affection of the world.

"They blame me for Dietz's death, but I didn't kill him."

"I know." She coughed. The strain was evident. She said, "I don't want to lose you like I lost your father."

"Me, neither," Oscar admitted. "I know what they did to my father. I wanted to ask you if it was true."

Carolyn nodded with a slight movement. For a few moments Oscar felt troubled.

"But there's something else you need to know," she continued, pain visible on her face. "Something that only your father and I knew. We had sworn never to tell you anything, but now I think it may be your only hope."

* * *

Your father and I met in Los Angeles at the end of the 60s. As you know, that was a very troubled time for society. The cold war was at its height. Most of the people spoke against the war in Vietnam. On the streets of California, hippies walked, proclaiming peace and free love. It was in those years that I met your father. Our love was intense and complete and to consolidate our relationship, in 1969, we decided to get away from that environment so we moved to San Francisco. There we got married. Dennis Brown was a very intelligent man and had gotten a job in a bank. His bosses knew how he could take advantage of that, so he soon ascended the chain of command.

One night in early 1970 we were walking from the supermarket with the week's provisions. Just one block before we got home, two men met us.

Both were armed, so your father held back. He and I were loaded with bags. The men searched Dennis, took his money, his watch and even his shoes. Then they searched me but didn't find anything of value. They said the money wasn't enough, thinking we were hiding more of it someplace.

I was going to scream when one of the men slapped me and threw the bags on the ground. He dragged me to the alley while his accomplice put the gun to your father's temple, telling him to walk behind us.

While one threatened Dennis and forced him to watch, the other one took advantage of me. They took turns raping me again and again.

The only thing I could do was cry, and every time I tried to scream in panic or pain, they'd slap me again. When that hell finally ended and both men were satisfied, Dennis, full of anger, saw the opportunity and struggled with one of them, until a shot sounded. The man fell to the ground, to the amazement of his partner. Without hesitation, Dennis raised the gun and shot the other one in the face. Then he knelt by my side, lifted me and carried me to the house.

When the police found the bodies and determined they were two criminals, they didn't try very hard to investigate further. We never reported the crime, and if any of our neighbors ever suspected us, they never told us.

Sometime later, the doctor confirmed the pregnancy and I became very sad, almost on the verge of madness. But your father swore to me that he would never think about the possibility that you were not his son. After all, it was impossible in those days to determine paternity and the truth was that there were probabilities that you were his.

He loved you and always wanted the best for you. It was for that reason that when he was offered the neo-Nazi deal in 1976, he said no. Your father was raised without his mother as she had died during labor. His denial was outright and without giving them the opportunity to convince him. That's why they killed him.

* * *

At the end of her story, Carolyn was exhausted. She found it hard to breathe. Oscar was crying on her chest. After a few minutes, he lifted his head a little and whispered.

"Why are you telling me this now?"

"Can't you see it, son?"

"What should I see?" he asked, surprised.

"Your hope! Your only hope. There's a chance you're not Hitler's grandson. You don't have to play their game or serve them at all. You can be free!"

Then he understood his mother's reason for confessing that story: there was a chance he was not Dennis Brown's son. Now he just had to find a way to prove it.

While his mind wandered in ways to prove paternity, a noise brought him back to reality.

The sound was the constant tone of the machine that monitored the heart rate of his mother. The machine was registering her as going flat-line. Oscar froze in fear. In less than two seconds several nurses and a doctor entered the room. There was chaos, everyone spoke quickly, and Oscar's little knowledge of French did not allow him to comprehend the conversation. A nurse kept pushing him out of the room while he shouted at her in English.

Finally, he found himself in the hall. Oscar closed his eyes and thought that his mother had only waited for him to give him news which could very well save his life. Even if she had to deny Dennis Brown's paternity, and he realized how painful this must have been for her. Sighing, he returned to the waiting room.

A few minutes later, he watched his mother being carried out on the stretcher, the sheet covering her face. He needed no further confirmation. He lowered his head and his eyes filled with tears.

CHAPTER TWELVE

The phone rang startling Nora Miller. "Hello?"

"Not sure you remember me, Nora. I'm Sergeant Frank Hagen. I work at the Metro."

"Yes, sergeant, I remember you."

"I'd like to chat with you. Can I invite you to have a coffee?"

Nora smiled. "I figured someone would want to talk to me sooner or later, but I didn't think they were going to send you, Hagen."

"Maybe they think it'd be better because we know each other from before," he joked.

"It's okay. In front of my office there is a café. I'll meet you about five o'clock."

"Thank you."

Nora ended the call and returned to work.

At five in the afternoon, Nora sat waiting for Frank Hagen. He arrived almost at a quarter past five. He looked agitated while he apologized for being late.

"I was about to leave."

"I wouldn't blame you for it. Thank you for waiting."

She courteously asked him about the reasons for the invitation.

The sergeant told her he had received calls asking about Oscar Brown. He could not reveal the identity of the people who called him, but she understood. Then he told her that this meeting was not official, that he had liked the young man when he met him and that he didn't think he was capable of the crimes of which he was accused.

"I don't think so either. Oscar has always been balanced, always in control of the situation. He's not prone to do irrational things."

"That's the impression I got from him, too."

"What do the police think?"

"Officially, I can't tell you, and you know it."

"Of course not," she agreed.

"But I will tell you that the problem is that he is on the run. It makes him look guilty even if he is not."

Nora was silent for a moment, thinking about the case, trying to see him analytically as a lawyer and prosecutor.

"There's another thing that bothers me. Oscar does not run away from problems. He confronts them."

"If he were to communicate with you...," Hagen didn't finish the sentence.

"Honestly, if he did, I don't think I'll come running to tell you."

"Yet, you're the District Attorney. You know better than that. It would make you an accessory to murder in the eyes of certain people."

"Yes, I know. But," Nora couldn't find the appropriate words to explain her feelings, despite having ended her relationship with Oscar so many months ago.

"Don't worry. I get it," he finally said.

"Do you know that his mother is sick?"

"Yes," Hagen replied.

Nora began to sob softly; the accumulated tension was having its effect and she could not contain it anymore.

"How long were you together?"

"More than two years," she said as she took a handkerchief out of her purse.

"You remember all the details, right?"

"Yes. When we met, he had a dog that I didn't like. He found the perfect solution and gave it to my sister's son. Now I cry every time I visit them."

"It's normal. On the other hand, you're still young and attractive. I'm sure you'll find someone."

"Thanks, Hagen. Really, it's been good for me to be able to discuss this with someone."

"Call me Frank, please."

"Okay, Frank"

"Now that I think about it, there's something I didn't mention to my superiors because I forgot to write it down. I had completely forgotten it, until now."

"What is it?"

"When I interviewed Brown, about his accident last year, he told me that the only thing he could see of the car that hit him was a Nazi flag. You know, the swastika and everything."

"Yes, he also told me about it."

"Did he say something more about it?"

"No. Actually, we didn't touch the subject much, and soon we separated. He went to Germany and I stayed here. Why?"

"I don't know. I thought it was curious about the flag, and then that he went to work in Germany." Frank sighed. "When you are a policeman, they teach you not to believe in coincidences, even though they sometimes happen."

CHAPTER THIRTEEN

The first thing that the Mossad agent managed to see was the ceiling. Because she did not have identification when she arrived at the hospital, Helga had been placed in the public room.

"Good morning, Helga."

She was startled to hear Oscar's voice. Her former boss looked different. His beard and mustache had grown. With the light coming through the window she could make out that his hair was no longer black.

"You have blond hair, Oscar."

"Oh, you noticed. Now my name is Günther."

She furrowed her brow and realized what had happened to her purse.

"So, you've used Günther's passport. Why are you still in the country? There was enough money to go far away."

"Actually," he said while smiling, "I left the country for a couple of days, but I came back for you, Helga."

"What do you want from me?"

"I need your help."

"I don´t understand. You know I tried to get you killed."

"Yes, I know that. The problem is you're the only spy I know. And now, more than ever, that's what I need."

She was surprised by the response. She knew that if Oscar had not put her in the taxi, she would have died on the street. She had neither the conviction nor the willpower to kill him. She was exhausted. And he knew it.

Helga listened as Oscar repeated what Carolyn Brown had told him before she passed away. She was amazed by Oscar's innate ability to act like a fugitive. She was even more surprised by the news that Dennis Brown was possibly not the man's father.

Helga concentrated on processing the information. After several minutes of reflection, she nodded. "All right. I'll help you although I can't see why you think you need me."

"It's very simple, really. I have to prove that I'm not Dennis Brown's son. I figured the best way is through DNA testing, but that is a dead end because they incinerated my father's body when he died in 1976. I know I am close to the key, but I can't find a way around that."

Helga searched her memories, rumors and gossips she'd heard over time. When she spoke, her excitement grew with each word.

"Look," she began, "you must go to the source. It's the best way, and probably the only one. Your problem is not being the son of Dennis Brown, but the grandson of Adolf Hitler. That is the kinship that you must annul."

"My father died twenty-four years ago, and I can't get samples from him. What makes you think that looking for something from Hitler would be easier? He's been dead for fifty years!" He said surprised.

"I can think of two ways. One, in Berlin, where there is a museum of World War II, and another in Russia."

"Russia?" Oscar asked.

"Yes. The Soviets were the first to arrive in Berlin, and the remains of Hitler's cremated body were transferred to Moscow. Joseph Stalin had Hitler's skull on his desk and proudly showed it to his visitors."

"I thought that was fiction."

"When the Mossad formed, one of the first missions was to find, capture or dispose of all war criminals. A lot of resources were invested, but we managed to verify that it was Hitler's skull that decorated Stalin's office."

Oscar felt a little relief, a glimmer of hope. The difficult thing would be to go to Moscow and get that skull. The Berlin Museum was ruled out because in Germany it would be very difficult to move about while the police were looking for him.

"You know," she added, "a couple of years ago we received a report from a guy who is contacted through the Internet. He could do it for a fee. He could go to Moscow and find what we need."

"Who are you talking about?"

"Nobody knows who he is. In the reports, they only described him as The Falcon."

* * *

Oscar rented a computer and put the ads looking for The Falcon on the Internet. Helga told him to include the words "Falcon", "please" and "luck" somewhere in the text of the ad. He'll then have to wait for him to communicate. For years he had been hunted, by several governments, but always the Falcon had the advantage of investigating the advertiser and, if something did not seem right, he would simply not respond. The Falcon always had the advantage.

Oscar made the first search pattern for the ads that included those words and was surprised to see more than a hundred. His odds were very low, but it was his best option at the moment.

He spent the night writing the ad that included the three keywords. He published it and went to a hotel. It was not the same one where he had been before going to France, but another, although in the same area.

Oscar, suffering more impatience than usual, checked his mail every two hours. An answer arrived on the second day. It was a coded message, inviting him to meet with the Falcon in an Internet chat place that would allow them to converse in private.

Punctual to his appointment, Oscar configured the computer with false data to access the site and after a few minutes, was online with the Falcon.

Falcon: What do you need?

Brown: It's going to sound crazy, but I want Hitler's skull currently residing in Moscow.

Falcon: What do you need it for?

Brown: I work at the University of Berlin and we want to run some DNA tests. As you can understand, we can't ask for it openly for obvious reasons.

Falcon: Sure. When do you need it?

Brown: As soon as possible. When can you have it?

Falcon: One week after I receive a deposit of two hundred fifty thousand US dollars in the account I'll detail below.

Oscar wrote down the account number, amazed at how simple the first contact had been. Soon he realized what was really going on. The Falcon still had the advantage. No money, no skull.

A heavy sense of uncertainty came over him. How could he know if it was not a premeditated scam or a trap? Helga or her associates may be out to rob him of his money as well as his life. He brooded for a moment and made the decision to take the risk. His life was worth more than the agreed price.

After triangulating some accounts and with the job of a stockbroker, he transferred two hundred and fifty thousand dollars.

Two days later, Falcon and Oscar reconnected to define the place of delivery of the package. Oscar gave him the address of a post office box in Paris. This arrangement was an emergency mailbox that Helga had. She had given him the address when they talked in the hospital and confirmed that it was what one of the keys Oscar had found in her bag was for. The other key remained a secret that she refused to divulge.

After the negotiations, Oscar returned to the hospital and, with a soft tone, ordered her to accompany him to France.

Without much opposition, she said, "I will go with you, but there is something I must do first."

"What would that be?"

"I need to report to my office."

"Do you think I'm going to let you tell them that I'm within your reach? Your mission is still to kill me, right?"

"My mission was to kill the descendant of Hitler. Now there's a chance you've got a reprieve. Also, I promised to help you, because I owe you my life. I always keep my word."

"So, what's the report for?"

"To begin with, the passport you are using is from my agency. If I don´t report that I have it or they think I lost it, they will put an international alert to prevent anyone else from using it."

"Hmm, they do not like to share their toys, huh?"

"Something like that. But do you see what I mean? I have to report to them so you can remain Günther."

"Alright. How are you going to do that?"

"When I get out of the hospital, we're going to get a public computer and I'll send them a message."

"What are you going to tell them exactly?"

"That I just got out of the hospital, that during a street altercation somebody wounded me with a sharp cutting weapon. That everything is in order, but I need a few days off and that I will be reporting weekly."

Oscar thought for a moment and finally nodded. He had no other options. He knew he needed the help of an expert. His luck as a beginner would not last forever.

That afternoon they released Helga. They avoided her place. They visited a small library that provided Internet service. They sat behind one of the computers and Helga connected to a mail server with a special identity. There were only two new messages in her inbox. The first was a confirmation that they had received their last message and that they should proceed with the plan. The second was a request for new reports. In this last mail she pressed the "Reply" button and wrote a couple of lines that did not make any sense, nor communicated anything she promised to say or not to say.

"What the hell is that about winter flowers?" he asked, annoyed.

Helga smiled. "They are predetermined keys. We use public servers for protection because we know how difficult it is to track billions of emails circulating on the Internet. But even so, in case they read something, we do not want them to understand anything."

"So, you write sentences that look innocent."

"Exactly. Gee, you do learn fast. Dietz was right about that."

"The fact remains that not knowing your codes, I can't know if you just betrayed me or not."

"You'll have to trust me."

"I have always believed that trust must work in both directions, and you already betrayed me once."

"Oscar ..."

"I know, I know. What do you want me to do? It's not easy to trust again."

"I understand. Let's move on."

They walked to the train station and Helga bought the tickets to Paris. The departure was in two hours, so they went to a small cafe to wait. Oscar bought a newspaper and read when they sat down.

"What are you looking for?" She asked.

"I want to know if the Government of Switzerland has found any connection between Gewinn and the bank that went bankrupt."

"Why should there be any connection?" She asked intrigued.

"Because just before you went in to shoot Werner, he made a call giving the order to set up the bankruptcy."

"How?" was all that Helga managed to sputter on hearing the news.

"He wanted to demonstrate the power they had in their hands. What better example than to break the second bank in Switzerland?"

Oscar told her the details of his conversation with Dietz. She hardly believed that Gewinn had that ability. It was power beyond what even the Mossad knew he had.

"I must report this to them," she said suddenly.

"At the moment, no. If you tell them this, they will know that I am within your reach. We hope to have some proof I'm not your man and then report it."

She accepted when Oscar told her it would be a test for him to trust her again.

They finished eating and returned to the station. The train left a few minutes after they had settled into their semi-private cabin. In front of them were a couple of elderly people holding hands.

"We're going to celebrate our fortieth wedding anniversary in Paris," the excited man informed them.

"I think that's fabulous. Congratulations," Helga told them.

"Thank you," the lady answered. "And you, newlyweds?"

"No," Oscar said so quickly that he surprised the couple. "This is just a business trip."

"Oh, how sad. I just said it because you make a nice couple," said the lady.

The long journey had tired Helga, who without noticing, laid her head on Oscar's shoulder. He supported her head and shifted his position to accommodate her. He ran his hand over his ex-secretary's black hair, caressing her. He looked up and found the old woman smiling sweetly but not commenting. At one, they arrived in Paris. Oscar and Helga rented a room. They had nothing more to do than to wait for any news of the Falcon.

CHAPTER FOURTEEN

The Falcon was in his little apartment. Sitting in front of the computer, he had just confirmed his acceptance of what would be his next job. He leaned back in his chair to think for a moment. He turned his head to appreciate the London autumn through the window. It was his favorite time of year. The fog gave him a sense of mystery and security.

Anonymity was a virtue in his line of work. His face was known only by a few people. However, he had a reputation for fulfilling his commitments on time. Apart from being an extraordinary thief, he was engaged in other tasks. He considered himself a person who obtained valuables for whoever hired him. In this case, his mission was to achieve something different, unusual: a genetic sample of Adolf Hitler. First, because the man had been dead for over fifty years; second, because history has always been inaccurate about the end of the Führer.

The popular version that Hitler committed suicide in the bunker and his subordinates burned his remains was the most accepted. Of course, among other rumors, the one that stood out the most was a possible escape to Argentina. The more the Falcon thought about it, the more he became convinced that he had signed up for a ghost hunt.

He got up, went to the window and looked at the roofs of London. His eyes turned east, towards Russia. His thoughts also took that direction. His client had mentioned the urban legend that tells that Joseph Stalin exhibited the skull of Hitler on his desk. Very proud, the communist leader showed it to his visitors, as an example to intimidate anyone who planned something against him. An effective trick. But Stalin died in 1953 and the Soviet Union disappeared in 1989, so where would he look?

He thought that there should be a museum in Moscow that kept the past glories of the communist leaders. So, without further ado, he figured out he needed the help of Jaime Porter.

Jamie was an archaeologist who studied the Mayan culture in Central America. The Falcon saved her life while he was working in that area. She was one of the few people who knew the true identity of the Falcon. They'd been in a romantic relationship for some time. He did his jobs and returned to Central America to be with her until getting the next contract. She accepted those conditions.

He padded back to his computer. He connected to the Internet and looked for the availability of flights from where Jamie was to London in the next few hours.

Five minutes later he dialed his girlfriend's direct number. When she answered, she asked him to excuse her because she was in a meeting and promised to return the call in a few minutes.

Those minutes turned into hours until finally, the telephone rang.

"You worried me. Who were you with?"

"At a farewell party for one of the groups of university students who do the practice in the archaeological sites. Don't worry, I'm back home now."

"And this time did anyone try to secure a recommendation by conquering you?" He knew he could trust her, but these games were fun for both them.

"Actually, yes. But I think he wanted something more than just a good grade. He kept inviting me to dinner!" she replied

"Well, I think he lost his chance. I need you."

"I think he did, too. I've missed you."

Falcon realized that she had misunderstood him, but he did not want to make her feel bad.

"How would you like to visit me in London? I even have a challenge for your inquisitive mind."

"Really? Hmm, sounds tempting."

It wasn't the time to fill her in on the details, and certainly not over the phone. However, he told Jamie that he had bought her a ticket to travel to London the next day. It was an electronic ticket and she just needed to go to the airline counter to claim it.

"I can't drop everything and leave immediately! Some of us have jobs with strict schedules."

"Oh, come on. Don't say that."

"Besides, how am I going to explain to Dad that my boyfriend calls me, and I run after him?"

Jamie's father, Bill Porter, was a retired commercial pilot who now lived in Central America. He enjoyed the company of his daughter later in life because in the formative years of the girl, he was serving a sentence in a federal prison in the United States. Bill knew his daughter's boyfriend by the name of Alexander Beck and believed him to be a vendor of equipment and computer programs. He was always kind to him, but he knew nothing of his double life.

"Bill is not going to bother you. Just don't tell him you're coming to meet me."

"I don't like to lie to him."

"It's not lying. Tell him that you will come to visit museums in Europe."

"And that's not lying?" She questioned him.

"Not this time. I told you I need you.

"Alex, what's up?" Jamie said worriedly.

"Trust me. Just come to London and I'll explain everything to you."

Jamie sighed before finally answering.

"Well, I think they owe me some vacation. How long do you need me?"

"Two weeks will be enough," said the Falcon, a little excited. They talked a few more minutes and then they said goodbye.

CHAPTER FIFTEEN

Like every morning, Jacob Goldberg arrived early at his office. He met his assistant in the hall who was waiting for him with the reports of what happened in the world.

"Anything important?" He asked as he left the briefcase on the side of the desk.

Jacob had a coffee maker that his staff always had prepared by the time of his arrival. The boss walked to the cabinet, took a large cup and filled it with the aromatic liquid. The office was immediately infused with the smell that pleased its occupant. For that reason, he kept a coffee maker in his office and not in the kitchen at the end of the hall.

"Nothing out of the ordinary. It was a quiet night."

"Good. No news is good news, eh?" Jacob said as he sat behind his desk and took the first sip of the only drug he consumed.

"There is an interesting thing, though. The agent we had in Frankfurt reported."

"When is she coming? She must give some explanation since they found her partner dead and we didn't hear from her until now. That's not protocol, and she knows it!"

"She suffered a knife wound in a street assault, as per her report. She was hospitalized for a few days. Since she arrived without papers the hospital admitted her in the general ward of the hospital as Jane Doe."

"She reported all that?"

"Yes. We also went through the hospital reports and they checked out."

"There is something that remains unaccounted. Is the objective?"

The director reflected. Hitler's grandson may have been the one who killed and wounded his agents. However, as a man of power, he did not take unsubstantiated actions. He kept silent for a few seconds, then asked:

"What about the documents and escape routes of her partner?"

"Everything is fine. She confirmed having them."

"Anything else happens in that case, you need to report to me immediately."

"Yes, sir. Anything else?"

"Not for now. Let me enjoy the rest of my coffee."

Once alone, Goldberg sighed. At least he knew she was alive. The director had a special affection for this agent for the efficiency and intelligence with which she resolved some operations previously.

He took one of the reports from his desk to keep up with his usual duties.

CHAPTER SIXTEEN

The Party's Convention in New York was a success. In the past two days, different speakers presented their opinions about why Paul Dieckens would be the best candidate to continue the work of the last eight years at the White House.

On its closing day, Vice President Dieckens knew his moment of glory had arrived. Sitting behind the scenes he listened to the announcer give the most relevant points of his twenty-five years of public life. The loud ovation told him the crowd was waiting for him.

He walked to the podium with confidence and poise, waving to the hundreds of acquaintances who cheered for him. He stood erect behind the microphones and began the acceptance speech he had prepared.

"Dear colleagues, I accept the nomination of the party with much appreciation." He paused for a moment while he was applauded by the audience. "I promise to take the necessary measures to continue with the economic boom that we have now" - another ovation. - "The opposition candidate proclaims family values as a prominent point in his campaign, accusing me of not having values because I was raised in an orphanage." -The crowd held its breath. Paul paused for a long moment to create expectation- "That's a low blow. He knows it, and many of his followers know it. Some of them have even called me to apologize and stopped supporting him. However, I tell you, if the candidate refers to lack of values due to lack of family, he is wrong. He IS wrong because I do have a family! I'm proud to admit I grew up in an orphanage because now I can call all Americans my brothers and sisters!"

* * *

Paul Dieckens acceptance speech was broadcast on radio and television in all parts of the world, causing different reactions. One of many spectators was the President of the United States, who observed him from the oval office with Chuck Mayer and Andy Pearson.

"I think we have a winner here!" Dean proclaimed, turning off the television. The small group settled into the armchairs in the center of the most famous political room in the world.

"With that speech, I think that more than some undecided already know how to vote next November," Chuck said.

"Now we can get back to work. How are we in Europe?"

"Nothing serious, Mr. President. The situation of Oscar Brown, presumed grandson of Adolf Hitler, got out of control. Very unusual for the Mossad," Andy, the Chief of Staff said.

"What happened?" The President asked.

Andrew related the events that occurred according to his reports: Oscar Brown is blamed for the death of Werner Dietz. This has also monopolized international news. However, Oscar Brown escaped.

"In addition, the one they believed was the real culprit in the murder of Dietz, a Mossad´s assassin, was found dead."

This news made the President feel apprehensive. Regardless of his supposed ancestry, Brown is an American, born and raised on this side of the Atlantic. Harding always had in mind the plaque on Liberty Island, which proclaimed "Give me your tired, your poor, your huddled masses yearning to breathe free."

No one in the oval room thought the quote referred to the heir apparent of one of the greatest tyrants of the twentieth century.

Finally, Pearson changed the subject of discussion to other national security issues of equal or greater importance than a single American in distress over his grandfather.

CHAPTER SEVENTEEN

Two days after their telephone conversation, Jamie Porter and the Falcon walked through their customs procedure to enter Russia. The Falcon had procured a passport and credit cards with the name of Michael Baker to travel with ease. One of the reasons why few people knew him was he was a master of disguise and had a vast number of documents that accredited him as a citizen of a dozen different countries in Europe and South America. Interestingly, he had no passport from the United States, his country of origin.

When leaving the airport, they went to the hotel. From there, going to a tourist agency, they signed up for a tour of the National Museum of History in Moscow. The Falcon had done his research online before coming.

The next day Jamie and Michael boarded a tourist transport that took them to the museum. With the credentials and the academic prestige of Jamie, they secured an interview with the Director of the museum.

Ivan Karpin was an affable man of more than fifty years. Blond hair and huge blue eyes that hid behind thick lenses set in black tortoiseshell frames. He welcomed visitors in his spacious and sober office. They talked for two hours, because the director was passionate about the Mayan culture, and pleased to converse with Jamie Porter, who had published several articles on the topic. It was one of the privileges that the director did not have often, so he seized the opportunity.

She told him about the many excavations she had led in Central America, particularly the discovery of a settlement in the Pre-Classic period, a study she published in the book "The Ancestors of the Mayans." This book, along with her other academic works, gave her an international reputation as one of the top archaeologists on the subject.

At that point, Karpin got up excitedly and walked towards a wall that was covered with books.

"That reminds me, I may not come by this opportunity again." Ivan returned to the desk with a copy of Jamie's book. "Would you be so kind as to autograph it? The photo doesn't do you justice. You're beautiful in person."

Jamie blushed to see her picture on the back cover of the book. She took it and confirmed Ivan used it more than a mere ornament. Several sheets were dog-eared and there was some wear and tear from the use.

The Falcon pulled out a fountain pen that he carried and offered it to Jamie. She signed the book without thinking much about the dedication and gave it back to its owner.

"Thank you. This book will no longer return to the bookshelf. I will buy another one for my use while I treasure this one."

Jamie exchanged looks with Michael Baker and seeing him smile, Jamie blushed again and ducking her head, took a deep breath and then added, "You know, it's not fair that you receive us this well and I will not leave you anything more than a signature in your book. If you give me the exact address of the museum, I'll send you another copy of my book along with others that you could share around the city."

"Whose books?" He asked with interest as he resumed his position behind the desk.

"One from my predecessor, John Newman. He was the leader of the project until he died. But he had published a couple of very interesting books. I have several copies. I will send them with pleasure."

"I think I heard of him before. Yes, you mentioned him several times in your book. Your admiration for him is remarkable. If you like them, I am more than sure I will love them. Thank you."

Little by little, Jamie was directing the talk to the section of Communism in the museum. She was interested, and after listening to Ivan speak for ten minutes about the exhibition, she dropped the question.

"Tell me something, but please do not make fun of me." She flashed him a disarming smile.

"Of course not," said the man in English with a heavy accent.

"I'm sure this may sound like a freshman question, but," she hesitated to continue.

"Yes?"

"Is it true that Joseph Stalin had Hitler's skull on his desk?"

Ivan Karpin laughed, but stopped laughing when he remembered his promise.

She smiled. "When I was studying at the university, I had a classmate whose parents were Russian, and she told me that and other anecdotes. I was curious and until now I have not had the opportunity to come. I can no longer stand the curiosity," she explained.

"Don't worry. It's a very common question. Stalin kept a skull on his desk and told everyone it was Hitler," said Karpin, smiling.

"And, where can I find out more about it?"

The man remained thoughtful for a moment and began to speak in a lower tone, as if in secret. "In '92, when the Kremlin wanted to remodel the institutions to remove any vestige of the previous regime, they sent us several boxes with things they did not think appropriate to throw away. Among them came Stalin's desk. When we checked the drawers, we found a skull and the little plaque with the name of Hitler. We decided that we could not exhibit either of the two things, so we consigned them to a warehouse," he concluded.

"And, would there be any chance of visiting the warehouse?"

The man shook his head. "That's in a special section of the warehouse. I still do not have a key."

Then Michael interrupted the conversation to ask the manager if he could give them a tour of the museum. They'd love him to be the guide. The man happily accepted and spent most of the day walking through the corridors, pointing out the different museum exhibits.

The museum was built at the beginning of the twentieth century. It had four floors. The first contained the reception area and administrative offices, and a quite extensive exhibition dedicated to the city of Moscow, from its foundation, development, changes through time with many black and white photographs.

The exhibition on the second floor was dedicated to Communism, but it covered not only the city but the entire country, throughout the eighty-year history of the regime. The exhibition on the third floor was dedicated to the Czarist era. A special niche showed the Romanov family and the little girl who was immortalized by the legend of her miraculous escape.

The fourth floor, closed to the public, was reserved for special exhibitions. Jamie proposed to him to bring samples of the Mayan civilization to make a temporary exhibition in the museum. The idea pleased the director so much that he wanted to go out and celebrate with a bottle of Vodka. Michael and Jamie apologized in the best way without offending their guide.

During the tour, they discovered that the building had a large basement that served as a warehouse. The Falcon managed to obtain several building diagrams designed to guide the lost tourists. Ivan Karpin pointed out the entrance to the basement and told them about the load elevator they had installed to be able to lower and raise large objects.

"Are those things safe? I always feel like I want to make visitors take off their clothes when something goes missing in my museum."

"We take good care of our property. Motion detectors in the rooms, cameras in the corridors. We even brought in an expert to make sure we had no blind spot."

"Why didn't you put motion detectors in the corridors too?"

"Oh, how I wish I could. But we have guards and they must make rounds. We tried the motion detectors in one floor as a test. Nobody could sleep that weekend because the alarm went off every five minutes."

The Falcon tucked away all the information in his mind while formulating a plan to enter and leave without being detected. If only he had a guided tour of every place that he had to break into.

They returned to the hotel to rest. The Falcon fulfilled Jamie's promise to have a day off in Moscow. They enjoyed the day exploring other areas of the city, bought some souvenirs with icons of Orthodox religious figures that also included some death cults. The Falcon had already worked out his plan for the next night.

On the night of the hit, the Falcon checked the equipment he had arranged on the bed: mountaineer's ropes, eyebolts, an air pistol that fired darts, sets of lock picks to open several types of doors and padlocks, a chronometer and night vision goggles, among other things. He dressed in all black: jeans, rubber shoes and a turtleneck shirt. The only garment of another color was a thick white coat.

Jamie was sitting by the bed watching him work, checking everything and then packing everything into a backpack. She admired the almost ritualistic process. She had seen him work in the past, but she was always surprised by his professionalism, even the seriousness in his face.

"How much are you charging for this job?" She finally asked

He answered smiling while putting away the last of the items. "A quarter of a million dollars."

"The sum seems reasonable, but the risk is also great."

"I thought it was a job with a simple linear sequence." He raised his gaze to her eyes. "The real payment was this vacation with you."

"Good answer. Hurry, I'll stay up waiting for you."

He obeyed immediately, picked up the last thing he needed to put in his backpack and walked to the door.

"Hey," Jamie called.

Falcon stopped with his hand in the doorknob and turned to look at her.

"Keep yourself alive," she said. It was a little tradition between them. Every time he went to do a job, she reminded him to stay alive.

This tradition had begun a couple of years before when they first met. The Falcon was about to submerge in an underground river. She told him and upon his return, he found an armed man about to shoot him while another man was about to rape her.

He smiled, opened the door and left the room. He went down the emergency stairs, to avoid suspicion. Once outside, he stopped a taxi. It was a few minutes before nine o'clock. He gave the driver an address that was several blocks away from the museum.

He got out of the taxi and walked the rest of the distance to the museum. The night air was freezing him to the bone. Moscow could be brutal in November. Upon arriving at the building, he passed by the front door and went on. At the corner, he turned into the alley that was between the museum and the neighboring building. In this wing were the service entrance, as well as a ramp on which trucks and containers loaded and unloaded merchandise.

However, the Falcon wasn't planning to enter through here. This was just the best place to climb the building. He stood in front of the door, took off his coat and opened his backpack. He pulled out a rope, secured it to the dart and inserted it into the air pistol. He looked up and pointed into the sky.

The shot was perfect. The dart reached the top of the building, falling on the roof. The tip opened like an anchor. The Falcon pulled the rope gently until the spikes hooked on the safety rail. Then the difficult part began. At thirty-three years old, the Falcon was in good physical condition, but climbing four stories in the middle of an icy night in Moscow presented a high degree of difficulty.

Minutes later, he reached the roof, unhooked the rope and stored everything in his backpack. He walked until he found the maintenance booth of the cargo elevator. The door had a double key. The Falcon took less than half a minute to open it. Once inside, he took the rope and tied it to the ceiling of the elevator shaft. He put on the repelling equipment and went down gently. He slid a few meters and checked the effectiveness of the brake. Just before starting the descent he put on his night vision goggles. The darkness of the shaft was total. He kept going down until he touched the elevator parked in the basement. Being a cargo elevator, it did not have a roof like the passenger lifts, so it was easy to land and open the basement doors.

This level extended throughout the length and width of the building, so there was plenty of area to search. The Falcon followed a predetermined pattern to cover the basement in the shortest possible time. Within ten minutes he found a restricted area, also locked. It took a little less than a minute to enter.

This inner section was a rectangular room about ten square meters. At the back, he found a wooden desk, with many boxes on top, but the drawers were facing the wall. The thief sighed and began to move boxes out of the way. Some were very heavy. Others seemed to contain only papers. He was finally able to move the desk away from the wall.

It was a luxurious piece of antique wood, carved cedar, owned by Stalin. He opened the drawers one by one. Many were empty. In the last one, he found what he was looking for. A human skull was placed on a base that sported a plate. The Falcon read the inscription:

"Adolf Hitler 1889-1945. Hated by everyone."

The last sentence was written in Russian, but the Falcon was able to read it. He carefully stored the skull in his backpack. He stood to replace the boxes as he had found them when he had an idea. He pulled out the skull and placed it on the desk. With tweezers, he extracted one of the teeth and, with a knife, chipped away a small bone fragment. These two samples were placed in a sealed bag. Then he took several digital photographs.

Fifteen minutes later he entered a taxi back to the hotel. Jamie, true to her word, was wide awake, awaiting his return. She was surprised that he had not brought the complete skull.

"Think about it. How can you pass that through customs? Even if you're a renowned archaeologist they might accuse you of being a grave robber. The tooth and the chip I removed should be enough to perform the study they want."

During the night, he carefully packed the skeletal remains, hiding them inside the souvenirs. The next day the Falcon and Jamie went to the airport to board a flight to Paris.

As they went through customs, Jaime was overtaken with anxiety. The Falcon hugged her and placed a tender kiss on her cheek. The customs clerk smiled distractedly and neglected to check their luggage too thoroughly.

Once in the city, they posted a manila envelope by ordinary mail with the skeletal remains, a few photographs, and a note.

CHAPTER EIGHTEEN

Three days after arriving in Paris, Helga Dystell felt much better. Her wounds had healed almost completely. Now she looked at Oscar Brown, a.k.a. Günther König, with new eyes. Not only for having saved her life, but for how efficient he had entered the spy game in such a short time. They shared a room in a cheap accommodation in the less touristy area of the city. Helga took the bed while he slept on the sofa. When she suggested that they had enough money for two rooms, he just shook his head.

"That's a good trick, but I'm not losing sight of you until I'm sure you're not planning to kill me anymore," he explained.

They waited anxiously for the closing time of the post office to waltz in just a few minutes before, which was the most hectic moment of the day. There would be less chance that the employees would notice the people coming and going.

"How did you decide to become a spy?"

"Excuse me," she said, somewhat surprised by the unexpected question.

"We have an hour to kill. I'm trying to pass the time in conversation."

"You sure know how to pick topics."

"It's better than talking about the weather," he teased.

"I spent two years in the national army. There I did aptitude tests and at the end of my obligatory service, they approached me to know if I was interested in studying these type of tactics. I was in the Mossad school for several years, in training. Then I was assigned small cases as tests. I have been a hundred percent operative agent for the last five years."

"How old are you, then?"

"I'm twenty-nine," she said. "But the work clothes and makeup made me look older."

"I had that thought, too," he said remembering his shock at seeing her for the first time without formal secretarial attire.

Helga shared details of her training and some tricks of the trade. Most people spent years of practice to master them perfectly, but Helga's intention was that Oscar had a correct notion of spy work and not the glamor they describe in movies and novels.

The time came. 4:45 pm. They crossed the street toward the post office. As foreseen, inside there were several people lining up for shipments and others opening the assigned boxes.

Helga and Oscar approached the one that corresponded to them, although the key's id number had been filed off as a precaution. Dystell knew the number of the locker.

They opened it and found a manila envelope. It was definitely not what they were expecting. Oscar took it out and read the name of the sender. It was The Falcon's agreed pseudonym.

They left the premises and returned to the hotel. They remained quiet all the way and waited until they arrived at the room to open the envelope. Helga made sure the door and the windows were closed, while the man they knew at the hotel as Günther König, sat on the bed and tore open the envelope.

He emptied the contents on the bed. There was a folded sheet of paper and two skeletal remains. When reading the note Oscar understood what had happened and congratulated the Falcon for preventing a difficult situation to explain. He read the letter again, this time out loud so that Helga could hear the contents and showed her the photos that were attached as evidence.

"The man's certainly a pro," she said.

"That's why you never catch him. Tonight's too late to visit the clinic. Early tomorrow morning?"

"Yes. Now move out of my bed, unless you want to trade."

Brown smiled and got up. He returned the pieces to the envelope and went to the sofa where he flopped down. The next morning, after a frugal breakfast, they left the hotel.

"How can you be sure that those bones are really Hitler's?" She asked as they walked.

"Look, I really have no way of knowing. I guess we'll ask for some evidence of antiquity in the bones. Hitler was born in the late nineteenth century so that will give us an idea."

"Then again, I think the photos looked convincing."

They had located a clinic on Rue Lecourbe on the first day of arriving in Paris. It was one of the most recognized laboratories in Europe.

They walked on the Rue de la Convention but turned to take the Rue Lecourbe. When they arrived at the clinic, they met with Dr. Lévêque. He was an affable man with black hair and an intense look. He didn't look a day older than thirty but when he spoke, he showed a lot of experience and security in what he said.

Helga handled the conversation with the doctor.

"We found these small pieces of bone in the backyard of the old house of my husband's aunt. We'd like to determine the kinship to know if they were the bones of his late uncle. You see, he was lost during the Nazi occupation."

The man understood this type of request very well and explained about the genetic traces and how to determine relationships.

"Obviously, the strongest and most common was from father to son, but in this case, a little peculiar, one could take the foundations similar to the grandfather-grandchild kinship that shared a certain genetic inheritance, although not as marked as that of father-son."

"I wish I could say I understood every word, but I'll just say I trust you," Oscar said.

Helga and Brown already knew all this because they had studied the subject before entering the clinic. Still, they pretended that they were listening to it for the first time.

Oscar gave him the remains he had gotten from The Falcon. The doctor called a nurse to extract a blood sample from Oscar's arm. Just to be on the safe side, the nurse also took a sample of his tissue and a few hairs.

While the samples were being taken, the doctor suggested they do an additional Carbon 14 test to the bones and determine their age.

"Good idea. Please do." Helga said.

After the nurse finished, Lévêque directed Helga to the financial department to pay for the services. When they were meeting in his office, the doctor told them that the results would be ready in about two weeks.

"That long!" Oscar exclaimed.

"I'm afraid so, monsieur. We must be careful with these tests," said the doctor.

Neither of them had considered that the tests would take two weeks. Oscar worried about having to be hidden for the duration. This was not part of the plan, but there was no other choice.

Thanking the doctor, they returned to the hotel. Along the way, he managed to get some national and international newspapers to determine how Oscar Brown's pursuit was continuing.

In them, he also read about the effects of the bankruptcy of the second bank of Switzerland, how the effects were felt during the following week. While the customers of savings accounts had their funds guaranteed by the government, the bank was engaged in many commercial deals ranging from insurance to credit cards.

Customers who had credit lines to work in their companies were suddenly canceled, leaving them with insufficient cash flow. Two of these companies had to declare bankruptcy because they could not reconsile at the end of the month for October. Another company sent hundreds of their personnel home with promises of a future settlement.

There were many customers who bore the shame of having their credit cards denied in establishments since the issuing bank denied the charges. Several of these clients kept only one credit card, and these were the ones who wrote letters to the Government of Switzerland complaining about their problems. Parliament appointed a committee in record time to investigate the causes and reasons that led to the bankruptcy of Bank Suisse Corp.

Oscar was horrified to think that he had witnessed the call that caused the bank's bankruptcy.

In Germany, news programs stopped transmitting Oscar Brown's picture after two weeks. They no longer saw the point of continuing with the same news. The police had become secretive about the case, and the last official statement was made at the end of Werner Dietz's funeral. The mayor of the city of Frankfurt attended the funeral and told the press that the city was mourning the death of one of its favorite children. Dietz's offices on the top floor of Gewinn were closed. However, the Gewinn Board of Directors met in an emergency meeting and appointed an interim president who could assume the basic functions of the company.

CHAPTER NINETEEN

The elections for the Presidency of the United States were scheduled for Tuesday, November 7. During the third week of October, the three customary debates were held with the candidates for president, in which Robert Dolger, the opposition candidate, hit several blows to Vice President Dieckens, but the quick and opportune responses of the latter succeeded. The media qualified him as the winner of the three matches.

The polls no longer showed Dieckens' almost certain victory as at the beginning of the campaign. Dolger had managed to close the gap, to such an extent that according to the latest polls, the election would be in the hands of the undecided who still did not know where to placce their vote. As never before, both campaigns focused on these citizens.

* * *

Goldberg leaned back in his executive chair as he read the reports from the previous night. The third report filled him with fury. He threw the reports on the desk and activated the intercom. The tip of his index finger turned white by the force with which he pressed the button.

"What the hell does that woman think she's doing? We don't pay for her to take a vacation in Paris!"

"She's following her target."

"Her orders were to report to me immediately. It's been too long now." The trust in his agent had overstepped the limits of his patience. "If she doesn't show up in two days, send a team after her."

* * *

On Monday, October 23, at four o'clock in the afternoon, a couple anxiously awaited the results of exams at a private clinic in Rue Lecourbe.

Finally, Dr. Lévêque called them to his office. Helga and Oscar took a seat in front of the doctor who already had the file at hand.

"I hope I did not make you wait long," he told them.

"No, we've only been waiting two weeks," Oscar said with a trace of sarcasm. "I hope it was worth it."

"I'm sorry, but I have bad news."

"Yes?"

"There is no indication of any level of kinship between the remains you brought and the blood test."

The doctor was surprised by the repressed emotion that illuminated the face of his client. It seemed that he was even happy about the result.

"Doctor, what about the carbon dating test?" Helga asked.

"Oui. That test dated the skeletal remains with someone who was born in the late nineteenth century and died in the forties."

Oscar clenched his fist in excitement. Helga and he talked with Dr. Lévêque about the exams for about twenty more minutes. They asked for the results in writing and the return of the bone samples.

Everything requested was delivered to them in a manila envelope at the reception desk. They left the clinic and returned to the hotel with a glimmer of hope stashed in an envelope.

"You see it? I'm innocent," he said.

"Oscar, I'm really sorry. I swear I'm going to help you get your life back."

They were in the room packing the clothes they had bought during the two weeks in the city. Although they did not believe that anyone was looking for Oscar in France, they changed their accommodation once a week as a precaution. In addition, Günther now looked nothing like Oscar Brown. The hair had grown enough to make another hairstyle, along with another application of bleach to maintain the blonde color described by the passport.

"What are we going to do now?" Helga asked.

Oscar could barely contain his emotion. His mother had given him one last hope before she died, and it had worked. Now he just had to communicate with the right people and get them to stop looking for him. He had enough time to plan this step while waiting for the results and he had it figured out.

One night, while his former secretary slept, he asked the operator for the telephone number and the address of the Metropolitan Police in New York. However, his intention was never to call. In reality, he had already chosen the recipient.

"We'll send a package to a policeman I met last year in New York."

Oscar told her about his accident the year before and how he had met Frank Hagen. Helga was interested in the facts, particularly when Brown confessed to her about the Nazi flag he had noticed on the front glass.

"I think that may have been Hoffman."

"Why?"

"He was the only one who knew who you were, apart from Werner Dietz."

Sitting on the bed, Helga took his hand. The spy's eyes were teary.

"Forgive me for ... for ... I do not know how to say it ..."

Oscar noticed the nervousness in Helga's cold hand, and felt his pulse quicken with anticipation. He placed his index finger on the woman's lips.

"It's water under the bridge." His tender tone was no more than a whisper. "Now help me get my freedom back."

Their gazes met. She came closer until she was right beside him. When her lips were only a breath away, she said, "I want to apologize to you."

"It's not necessary."

"Yes, yes, it is."

Helga kissed him. Her lips were soft. Her tongue made way, parting his lips, exploring. Oscar stroked her back until he found the buttons on her blouse. With great care, he unhooked them, one by one.

That night they made love for the first time. Helga was sure that Oscar was not a descendant of that genocidal monster and only then she could unleash her feelings. She went to sleep with a satisfied smile across her face.

The next day, and on the advice of Helga, they took a train to Luxembourg. When they reached the small principality, they looked for an international courier office. From there they sent the sealed package to Frank Hagen.

The original plan was to return to Paris the same night, but in the end, they decided to take a room in one of the best hotels in the city.

* * *

Frank Hagen tried to clean his desk as quickly as possible so he could leave early on Friday. A few minutes before five, an employee of a shipping company arrived. "Mr. Frank Hagen?"

"Yes?" said the policeman, looking up.

"I have a package for you. Please sign here," he said, extending a clipboard.

Hagen, already with the envelope in his hands, checked the name of the sender. He was surprised to see that it was Oscar Brown, from Europe. Without hesitation, he opened the package and found a smaller envelope inside. In addition, there was a single sheet of paper folded, printed on one side.

Upon reading it, Hagen had a summary of everything that had happened to Brown in the last month: how they had kidnapped him to tell him who he was; how operatives from another country killed Werner Dietz and left enough evidence to incriminate him;

about the confession of his mother, and about obtaining bone remnants of Hitler to do the DNA tests; of how Gewinn had engineered the bankruptcy of Bank Suisse Corp.

In the last paragraph, Oscar confirmed that he was hiding in Europe and explained that the additional envelope contained the results of the biological samples obtained. He requested his help so that the Government could carry out the tests that they may consider pertinent but that would help him because he was an innocent American citizen involved in such an international mess. He also instructed Hagen about an electronic address where they could send him messages.

Astonished by everything he had just learned, he thought of calling Nora Miller and telling her what had happened. But in the end, he decided first to tell a friend that he worked with from the FBI.

This friend showed interest in the story that Hagen had confided in him. They met that same evening and the policeman gave him the information.

CHAPTER TWENTY

Andy Pearson received a phone call from the Director of the FBI explaining the situation of Oscar Brown; the letter that Frank Hagen had received in New York and what he planned to do about it.

"Run your own tests? How?"

"Easy. I understand that Oscar Brown had to look for Hitler's remains in Moscow, but we were a little more efficient about it. We also obtained blood samples from Brown in a hospital."

"And?"

"Well, I'll let you know when I have the results of the tests and compare them with the ones he sent us."

"Perfect. Keep me informed."

"Of course."

Pearson ended the call. It was Monday morning and several reports of what had happened in the world during the weekend still awaited him.

* * *

The United States celebrated Halloween in the middle of a presidential race for the White House. The elections were a week away and there were many voters undecided.

During this week, Robert Dolger was made aware of all the situations that were happening worldwide by the Director of the CIA. Among the much data that they discussed, the theme of the American wanted by the German police stood out. He was also wanted by Interpol throughout the rest of Europe, accused of the murder of one of the richest men in the world.

"Did he do it?"

"We'll never know for sure. The police say they have enough evidence. However, he contacted us to ask for help."

"What should our response be?"

"The jury is still out. Well, in this case, the President hasn't made a final decision."

"The United States Government will not protect criminals. Tell that to Harding."

"Remember that no one is guilty until proven otherwise," the Director said.

"Perfect! Let him prove it first!"

* * *

The FBI had the most sophisticated criminology laboratories in the world. DNA testing in a commercial clinic would take two weeks, but the Feds could get results in less than four days.

The doctor handling the samples did not know anything about the case he was studying. He had received the samples marked with maximum confidentiality stamps. He proceeded with diligence but performed blind tests to be on the safe side.

He analyzed the hair samples. Using the proper equipment, he obtained a report of the genetic fingerprint that made this sample unique. He followed the same procedure with the blood sample. In the end, he was able to compare both results to make the kinship deductions that were requested.

By Thursday afternoon he had already delivered the results to his supervisor, who promptly forwarded them to the FBI

Director. After the reports were filed, they were bound to secrecy and didn't—in fact they couldn't—discuss the case with anyone.

* * *

On Friday at noon, President Harding, Chuck Mayer, Andy Pearson, and the directors of the FBI and the CIA met in the Oval Office. The case they dealt with was delicate. Oscar Brown had gone from being an American wanted as a suspect in a foreign country, to a fraud case, and potential embezzlement with illegal trading thrown in for good measure. After all, the financial collapse of Bank Suisse Corp would bring repercussions to the United States soon.

"What have you discovered about the bank?" the President asked.

"Nothing so far," the FBI Director replied. "We always suspect the possibility that someone was involved, but we would never have thought of Gewinn as guilty."

"What do you think?"

"I'm leaning toward it could be possible, albeit hard to believe. Yet, we can't prove it."

"What about Brown?"

"We have genetic fingerprinting results, but ..." the director was interrupted by Chuck Mayer.

"The ones he sent us?"

"Yes, as a starting point. We double checked everything. We obtained residual blood samples at the New York hospital where Oscar Brown was admitted last November for a car accident. We asked help from our cousins in the CIA to get samples from Hitler. They supplied us with the samples in less than two days."

"Well done!" The president told the director of the CIA.

"Thank you, Mr. President. It wasn't that difficult, to be honest. There's a museum in Berlin where there are several objects that belonged to Hitler. One of our operatives obtained the samples and sent them through the diplomatic bag the same day we requested them."

"Well, I congratulate you twice. Not only for efficiency, but for the spirit of collaboration."

"In conclusion," the FBI man retorted, "both tests turned out to be negative. Oscar Brown does not have any kind of genetic relationship with Adolf Hitler."

"Can Oscar Brown help us get evidence to expose Gewinn?" the chief of the National Security Agency asked.

"I guess so. Truth is we won't know until we make contact and ask him directly."

After a few seconds, President Harding took the floor to conclude the issue. "Gentlemen, this settles the argument. A fellow citizen of the United States is being unfairly persecuted by foreign powers. It is our sworn duty to protect him."

The heads around the table nodded. All but one. The President chose to ignore it.

"It's time to bring our boy home. Make it happen."

* * *

With the approval of the President, a plan took shape. Pearson led the initiative as the FBI would cover the legal field and provide Oscar Brown the opportunity to enter the Witness Protection Program. This was a vital program designed to protect key witnesses who had risked their lives to prosecute and convict criminals.

Pearson asked the CIA to establish contact with Oscar Brown and offer him a new identity in exchange for the evidence to expose Gewinn. At the same time, they would communicate to the Mossad the biological results so that they could withdraw the death sentence imposed on Brown.

Once Brown had accepted the terms, the Justice Department would be the one in charge through the diplomatic corps to communicate with the authorities of Germany to inform them about the conspiracy against Oscar Brown, since he was trying to expose the illicit deals of Gewinn that could have led to the bankruptcy of Bank Suisse Corp.

CHAPTER TWENTY-ONE

Oscar reviewed the inbox of the email address he had established to communicate with the government. He got an answer on Saturday.

His instructions were to meet someone, he assumed a spy, to receive a formal offer of the help that the US government was willing to supply.

"There would be conditions, of course," Helga said.

"Obviously. But I'm a guy on the run, wanted for murder. What could they possibly want from me?"

"Maybe proof to bury Gewinn."

"If that's the case, then I'm screwed. I don't have anything."

"That's not entirely accurate. There's plenty of information in your email. You can access it remotely, remember?

"One, if the people from Gewinn are half as smart as Dietz said they were, they'd have that email purged. Or worse, set it to track me down."

"I love how you're thinking as a fugitive. Didn't take long. You're a natural."

"It's not that. Think about, if they think I'm Hitler's grandson, I've been running away from that all my life."

"You're right," she said.

"Still, I'll need your help tomorrow."

"Doing want?"

"They want me to arrive alone, but that doesn't mean you can't watch out for me from a distance."

"That I can do."

Right after dawn on Sunday Oscar walked alone through the Champs de Mars, at the foot of the Eiffel Tower, with a copy of the New York Times in his right hand. This was the signal that had been indicated to him to be recognized.

"Mr. Brown?"

"Yes?"

"Good Morning. I'm Larry Smith, I work with ..."

"The CIA?" Brown interrupted.

"God, no! I'm the United States' Ambassador to France."

If not a CIA operative, Oscar had expected a secretary, or a guard. Not, the top dog in France. He was impressed.

Larry Smith was a tall man, with green eyes and brown hair that feathered into white on the sides. His pronounced waist denounced his taste for French cuisine. He was dressed in an expensive gray suit, a light blue tie and white silk shirt.

"I wish to thank you for coming to this meeting. My instructions are to apologize on behalf of the government for not having acted sooner. Now we received orders from the very top to make you a priority. The White House is willing to do everything possible to help you."

It sounded too good to be the true. Oscar could hardly believe it. Sarcasm slipped into his thoughts. They must have checked his tax record and determined he was worth saving, if only to preserve the steady income from taxes.

"Did they bring you up to date about my situation?"

"Yes. I was informed last night. I must admit that at first, I thought it was a joke."

"Honestly, me too."

The two men walked until they found a cafe across the street from Champs de Mars. Its outdoor table would give them the privacy of hiding in plain sight.

After the waiter took their order, Oscar turned to Mr. Smith. "Let's hear it. What's the deal?"

"It's quite simple, really. Let me tell you that more than two government agencies collaborated to put this deal together. First order of business is that we need to know if you can get hard evidence against Gewinn about the bankruptcy of the Bank Suisse Corp."

There it was. Helga had been right. He came with no evidence, but at least with a prepared response.

"At this point, I don't know what I can get. What happens if I say no?"

"The FBI will provide you with a new identity anyway. You'll be able to live in peace wherever you want. The catch is you'd have to live in hiding. You see, the information would be useful to negotiate with Germany to withdraw their arrest warrant and with Switzerland to proceed against Gewinn."

Their order arrived. Oscar's coffee tasted a bit like freedom.

"That means I could get out scot-free. Even keep my name if I want, my career, all of it."

"If you feel so inclined."

Oscar Brown looked thoughtful. The plan had the appearance of being the light at the end of a dark tunnel. Perhaps he could end this nightmare. He thought about it for a few minutes enjoying the coffee.

"I would have to go back to Germany first, and see what I can get in Werner's office."

"I must warn you of something."

"What is it?"

"We can't negotiate with the Germans until we have obtained the evidence. If you go back now, you could be captured, and we could not do anything. Do you understand?"

"I believe the risk is worth taking. I have a lot to gain if I find something useful."

"You're right about that. When you get the evidence, you can contact me at this number," he said and handed him a business card. "I'll make sure you get safe passage back to the United States."

"Looks like we have an agreement. Thank you, Mr. Smith."

Oscar got up and dropped a few Francs on the table to pay for the coffee. Then he hurried away.

He was impressed with Helga's abilities. She said he wouldn't see her, and he never spotted her. Yet, he felt confident she was standing guard over him.

Her skills would come in handy when they returned to Frankfurt.

* * *

On Sunday afternoon Oscar and Helga were sitting in a private cabin on a train to Germany.

"But what do you think you'll find?"

"The hell if I know. They asked me for some proof of what Gewinn did, just as you guessed it. The best place to look for that is Werner's office."

"You think he left some trail that would incriminate him?"

"One can only hope. I must try something. Have you read the newspapers? Have you seen the problems caused by bank failure? I feel responsible."

"Why? You didn't have anything to do with that," she said.

"I feel guilty because it was an example that Werner wanted to give me. An example of the power he had. He was trying to prove something with this. In a way, it was his sales pitch. He wanted me to join the cause."

Helga sighed. She knew it would be impossible to talk him out of it. Her best course of action was to help him. She owed him that much. They'd come prepared with another ace up their sleeve.

CHAPTER TWENTY-TWO

The train arrived right on time. The passengers disembarked without major complications. Among them walked a couple holding hands.

Brown accompanied Helga, who still hadn't revealed her real name, to a row of lockers. She opened box 508 with the key she carried. Inside were two backpacks. Helga took both and gave one to Oscar, then closed the locker and they walked out of the station.

They went to a small hotel a few blocks away. Once in the room, Helga emptied the contents of both backpacks on the bed.

Money. A lot of money, two passports and two weapons. One was a six-shot .38-caliber revolver. The other was a semiautomatic pistol manufactured in Belgium, 9 millimeter and capable of fourteen shots.

"Why are there two types of weapons?"

"My partner was a fan of revolvers. He dreamt of being a cowboy. A six-shooter complimented that ambition. This was his personal weapon. The other is mine."

"Do you know how to shoot a revolver?"

Helga's glance was a sufficient response. She continued with the cleaning of the weapons. Then she loaded the ammunition that also came in the backpacks.

The normal time of the start of operations of a company dedicated to the stock market as Gewinn was nine in the morning. Therefore, at five thirty on a Monday the offices would be deserted.

* * *

Just across the street from the Gewinn building was a parked car, with the engine off. A man waited inside. He watched the couple approach the building but did nothing.

* * *

Helga and Oscar found the place locked down like a fort. Oscar keyed in his password and the electronic panel blinked red. No access.

Helga tried her own password, "Maybe they overlooked the little people."

"I never overlooked you."

The panel blinked red again. "Apparently they didn´t either," she said.

"May I help you?" A male voice said from behind, startling the couple.

"Who the hell are you?" Oscar said, faking bravado and hoping the thundering beat of his heart wasn't visible.

"A stranger offering to help."

"Are you security? I don´t see a badge."

"I don't have one as I´m not with Gewinn. On the other hand, had I planned to hit the place, I would've procured one."

"Criticizing is not the same as helping," Helga said.

"You know, for a Mossad agent, you´ve taken this case very far with just thoughts and prayers."

"Who sent you?"

"There you go, the most cliché question in the book. Yet, I reckon you´d like to know. The truth is nobody sent me. I´m here of my own accord because I took an interest." He walked away and signaled them to follow him.

They went around the block to the parking entrance. There was a pedestrian access door.

"The problem with certain people, architects in particular, is that they put too much thought into front appearances and neglect the back." The man fished out something that looked like lock picks from his coat pocket. "They installed this door as a last-minute addition, very late in the construction, when budget ran thin. No money for an electric panel, what do they do? They used a regular lock."

He worked the lock in under a minute. "Come on," he said.

Oscar hesitated at the door. Why should they trust a stranger? He traded a look with Helga who shrugged. She didn´t know what to do either.

"Well, come on. Whatever information you´re planning to steal from Werner Dietz is not gonna come to you."

"Who are you?"

"I´m a friend of the friend you hired to visit Moscow. He was curious about your case and shared the information with me."

"Damn Falcon has no respect for privacy."

"Haven´t you ever heard there´s no honor among thieves? Now, don't say his name out loud. He can only survive living as a ghost. Now, like I said earlier, I took an interest in your case. I think I can help so here I am."

Helga took the first step. Still doubtful, Oscar decided to trust Helga´s instincts and followed her.

They walked down the corridor until they reached the bank of elevators. Helga pressed the call button before she realized the man had walked by and continued down the hall.

"Always assume they're expecting you. If you use the main elevator you might as well ring ahead and ask them to have coffee and donuts ready." The stranger smiled at his own joke, then he looked amused at the lack of response from Oscar and Helga. "This way to the service elevator none of the building tenants know about."

"How come you know?" Oscar asked.

"I told you already. I prepare more than with just thoughts and prayers."

"Do you have a name? What do we call you?"

"Call me Jesus, for I´m your savior."

"The hell I will," Oscar said.

"Suit yourself."

They reached another locked door that delayed them no more than thirty seconds. The German word for private appeared stenciled on the door.

Bare walls greeted them inside the room, another striking difference to the opulent front foyer. This entrance was for less important people that didn´t have to be impressed. The sparse furniture was comprised of a plain secretarial desk with a chair, a closed log book, and nothing else. A hallway led them to another elevator bank. There were two instead of the six in the front.

The three boarded the elevator and rode to the top floor while soft instrumental music came out of the top speakers.

"Well, at least they torture them with the same music as the front," Helga said.

Oscar turned to see her. The strange man cracked a smile. The stranger. Oscar decided to refer to him as Jay. Not his savior, but a wannabe with the same initial.

They got out at the top floor and entered a hallway Oscar wasn´t familiar with.

"I´ve spent a year of my life in this building. I thought I knew every nook and cranny."

"You know, every time you took off in one of your little exploratory adventures people gossiped you were sneaking out to smoke."

"Office gossip is inevitable, I guess." They reached the lobby, then the anteroom to Werner´s office. The offices of Werner Dietz were at the end of the corridor. There was a closed glass door that needed a special key to open. Oscar tried his key, but it did not work.

Jay came up to the front and punched in the key code. His hands were gloved. The light changed from red to green.

"One of Werner's assistants is very old. She writes down the key code they give her every week on a small black book she keeps in the center drawer of her desk."

"What the hell?" Oscar turned to see the man as he raised his hand to show the little book. Then he understood. Jay had ransacked the desk while Oscar keyed the wrong code.

Heir of Evil

"Helga, I have a question for you. You never appeared on the news, not even after the police found that dead partner in your apartment."

"The apartment was not in the name of Helga Dystell, so the police failed to make any connection."

"You're full of surprises," Oscar said.

"That's the job."

Oscar pushed the door and they entered.

The door to Werner's office posed no challenge. Upon entering, they noticed that the curtains were pulled back and tied. The corner office sported an impressive panoramic view of Frankfurt am Main. Several landmark buildings filled the view, and the background was graced with River Main.

Werner's desk was a huge piece of precious wood lacquered in black. A solitary phone sat at one end and a computer at the other.

Oscar sat down in the black leather chair and turned on the machine. A box asking for username and password appeared on the screen.

"I don't think we thought this all the way through."

"That's what I've been telling you," Jay said.

"Let me try." Helga replaced Oscar in the chair and began to press keys. Suddenly, the screen went black. Soon the blank command line appeared. The woman continued to type, and the image changed again, this time listing files.

"The spy training also turned you into a hacker?" he said with admiration.

Helga shrugged as she continued working with the computer.

Twenty minutes later, and after several blind alleys, Helga found something.

"Look at this."

He peaked at the screen filled with what appeared to be a ledger. "What is it?"

"It's a listing of Dietz's personal files. He kept them hidden. I had to change the properties of the general directory to access them."

"Would it bother you to explain that to me in English?"

"There's no time for a class. What's worse, I don't know if it's what we're looking for. My hunch is that if Dietz hid them then they must be important."

"Makes sense."

Helga opened several documents at random and read them quickly.

"This is very interesting. Let me save a copy."

Oscar pulled a usb memory stick out his shirt pocket. He put it in the slot and Helga started copying the files.

Oscar read some of the information and whistled.

"This is more than what we were looking for. What are you going to do with that information?" Helga asked.

"Nothing for me to do but pass it along. At least I fulfill my part of the deal. I'll take this to Smith and see what happens."

"Who's Smith?" Jay wanted to know.

"Um, he's my contact with the government."

"What contact? What did you do?"

"I made a deal. They will help clear me if I give them information on Gewinn. Smith is my contact."

"Are you sure he's legit?"

"What do you mean?" Helga asked.

"Well, anybody can pose for a government agent and offer you a deal. Then kill you when you deliver it. Let me ask again, do you have proof?"

Oscar looked straight at the man. He appreciated the help the man had provided. Jay was the reason they had come so far. However, he didn't like the patronizing tone, nor the attitude. He had checked Smith out and confirmed his identity.

He was about to admit as much to Jay, but then he thought better of it. "I know Smith as much as I know you. If I trust you, I have to extend him the same courtesy."

"Touché."

"The file transfer is complete," Helga said.

Oscar took out the stick and dropped it into his pocket. At that moment the front door opened, revealing the silhouette of a man advancing towards them. As they looked up, they could see who it was.

"Dietz! You're alive!"

"No thanks to you." Werner Dietz stood framed by the door in an immaculate suit, as usual. This time he also had a Luger in his hand. "Alas, I can't really blame you, Oscar Hitler."

CHAPTER TWENT-THREE

Oscar eyed Jay who, for some reason, didn't look surprised. The stranger sat down on the couch as if preparing to see a play.

"What are you planning to do?" Oscar asked.

"Nothing for now." He lowered the gun and walked to the desk behind which the couple was and directed them to the couch. The three of them crowded onto the furniture. Helga sat in the middle, her hands on her lap.

"Who the hell are you?" he pointed the gun a Jay.

"Nobody important, I just helped them break into the building."

"You found that easy?"

"Exceedingly."

Oscar turned to face Jay. "What do you mean, easy?"

Werner smirked. "He's right, Oscar. I was expecting you. At least I was expecting you alone, but you brought a gang. It's a shame the girl's a Jewish rat. She was the best secretary who worked in this company."

"But, but ... I saw you ..." Oscar couldn't finish saying what he thought.

"Dead?" his former boss said. "Everything was a play. I received a report of what the Jews were thinking, and I took precautions. We agreed with the police to continue the farce of my death to capture you."

"Bulletproof vest?"

"Of course. Now I always use one. I had to buy new suits so that it would not show. What do you think of that, Herr Hitler?"

"I'm not Hitler's grandson!" He screamed. The sole idea repulsed him.

"What the hell are you talking about? Of course, you are."

"No, that's not true. I have evidence."

Dietz did not understand Brown's babbling. What could he be talking about? In the end, he decided to investigate a little more thoroughly before killing the girl.

"Explain, then."

Oscar looked at the floor as if gathering his thoughts. Helga's hands fell from her lap to her sides.

"My mother was raped by some thugs when she was newly married. My father and she never went to the police. I couldn't do the DNA test with my father because you killed him. He was cremated."

"Yes, I was there at the funeral parlor. I remember wishing he'd burn in hell. Watching the cremation made me think my wish was granted."

"You son of a bitch!"

"Anyway, you couldn't test with your father, so what did you do?"

"We got Hitler's DNA and I took the exams. They came out negative."

"It cannot be," said Werner surprised.

"That was always the problem with the Nazis. You guys never accepted the truth even when it spat in your face," Jay said. His tone casual.

Dietz smiled, a wicked smile. His mind had focused on another possibility.

"You mean you're a bastard?" His look reflected contempt.

"Better to be a bastard than being the grandson of one." Oscar kept his face straight, hoping to project his conviction and anger at Dietz's contempt.

"If that's the case, then we do not need you anymore."

Slowly, he raised the gun. His finger was on the trigger and he began to slowly squeeze. A split second before the gun fired, a deafening noise filled the office. The explosion was close to Oscar's ear. He clapped his hands to the sides of his head.

Oscar watched Dietz's right eye disappear as he fell dead to the floor. With his hand pressed hard to his head, he tried to alleviate the intense pain in his ear. He felt a warm liquid emanate from the canal, then realized that his eardrum was bleeding.

He turned to see Helga. She was holding the revolver in her hand. She had removed it from his waist while he and Dietz argued. Realizing his intent to kill them, she fired first.

This time she had aimed at his head. Dietz had made the mistake of revealing his advantage.

"Mission accomplished," she said after a sigh.

"We have to get out of here."

He went to the desk and picked up the phone, took out the card the Ambassador had given him and dialed the number. Somewhat surprised to hear the voice of the American answering, he informed him of what had just happened.

"I have enough evidence to expose Gewinn."

"Are you sure, Brown?"

"I am. But I still have other news."

"Tell me."

"I found some confidential information describing Gewinn's operations in the United States. Werner has a contact informing him of everything, so he knew that the Mossad would try to kill him."

"That's impossible."

"I know who the contact is."

"Who's the mole?"

"I can't and won't tell you over the phone. What's more, I will not tell anyone other than President Harding."

"Are you crazy?"

"I'm standing right next to the heir of the evil Nazis with his head exploded to bits. Maybe I'm a bit crazy. That doesn't change the importance of the information I've got. Send your people to fix this disaster."

"Let me see what I can do."

"I'm going to the American consulate here in Frankfurt. Arrange to establish a secure line of communication so I can talk to the President."

"I can't order President Harding to talk to a civilian just because you want him," Smith sighed.

"Believe me. The President will not regret having talked to me." Oscar hung up the phone.

Helga and Jay stood looking at him in awe.

"You drive a hard bargain, Mr. Brown."

"Yeah, well. You don't know what I know. You didn't read the files."

"Care to bring me up to date?"

"Not a chance. This is sensitive information." He smiled. "I didn't trust Smith with it. I won't trust you either."

"Fair enough." The man looked around the room until his gaze fell on Dietz's corpse still twitching on the floor. "I think my job's here is done. You can find your way out on your own."

Just as he had come, the stranger left.

"I think he's the Falcon," Helga said.

"Why do you think that?"

"You know how people keep asking stupid things, for a friend. Yet you never get to know that friend."

"Gotcha."

They walked to the door of the office, leaving on the carpet the now motionless body of the man who wanted to kill him.

When they reached the elevator, Oscar realized that he could not stand to be in such a confined space.

"Let's take the stairs."

They walked to the end of the hall, down the emergency stairs and left the building. A cool breeze caressed his face.

As they crossed the street, Oscar and Helga turned to see a car barreling towards them. In the last instant, Helga pushed Oscar out of the way and took the brunt of the hit.

Oscar fell by the sidewalk and turned in time to see Hoffman speed away.

"Helga!" He rushed to her side.

Her breathing was ragged. She had a nasty cut on her face and her arm twisted at a wrong angle.

"I have to get an ambulance."

"It's already too late." Her breathing was slow.

"Helga... don't leave me now. I have proof. We can be together now."

"How I wished we could."

"Helga."

Her eyes looked dazed, the life melting away from them. "My real name is Ruth." A smile lit her face. She closed her eyes, took a final breath and died.

His feelings for his former secretary had changed over the last few days. She had been tasked to set him up or kill him. She almost succeeded in her mission. When confronted with the truth, she chose to switch camps. Oscar realized he had forgiven Ruth even before she died to save him. He was amazed at how quickly he had accepted her real name.

He didn't want to abandon her on the street, yet he knew he couldn't afford to wait for the authorities to show up. The German police still had a valid warrant for his arrest.

It pained him to leave. He stood up and looked at both sides of the street. The early morning traffic hadn't started. It wasn't even six. The streets looked deserted.

He spotted Jay standing on a corner, looking sad. The man shook his head and mouthed, "I'm sorry."

Oscar responded with a gentle nod.

Jay turned and disappeared around the corner.

Oscar knew he had to do the same. He turned in the opposite direction. He took one step, then another. His feet seemed to know where to take him. That was good because at that moment he wasn't sure.

He doubted he'd ever be sure about anything else in his life. He continued down the street. In the distance, he heard the sirens of the patrols that were coming to surround the entrance of Gewinn. At least Smith had gone ahead and done his job.

Oscar went his way without even caring for the patrols. He felt as if he was about to wake up from a nightmare. He was innocent, damaged but innocent. He carried the proof of his freedom in the usb stick inside his pocket.

He'd be alone, but free. He may never be Oscar Brown again, but at least he felt sure he'd never be Oscar Hitler.

His ordeal was almost done. There was only one more thing to do.

CHAPTER TWENTY-FOUR

Jacob Goldberg sat in his office after receiving the news from his Chief of Operations.

"Are you certain?" He asked when he finished.

He nodded. "The FBI sent us a copy of the results of the DNA tests, as well as the methods used to obtain the samples."

"And you believe them, obviously."

The subaltern nodded and added, "The best thing of all is that the real Nazi, Werner Dietz, did die this time."

"Okay, inform them that Oscar Brown is safe from us. But how did we fail the first time? We have one of the best teams in the world."

"It was an operational error. Our agents failed to anticipate that Werner could be wearing a bulletproof vest. I already gave instructions so this will never happen again."

"What did you do?"

"The new standard procedure calls for them to verify that the target is dead."

"Coup de grâce?"

"If necessary. They should aim for the head on the first try, though."

"All right. However, we lost two agents in this operation. I don't like that."

"Me neither. By the way, I already canceled the passports and credit cards that were assigned to them."

"Good. What else? You look like you have something to say but don't want to."

"That's correct. We received a letter."

"From whom?"

"Oscar Brown, of all people. Our agent must have instructed him on how to contact us."

"Well, what did he say?"

"You better read it for yourself." He passed a folded piece of paper to his boss.

Goldberg and his chief of operations discussed the letter and several other issues of Mossad operations before the meeting ended. When the chief of operations left and Jacob was left alone in his office, sitting behind his desk and taking his second cup, he sighed thoughtfully.

"At least now there is one less Nazi in the world. Sometimes I feel we will never finish eradicating them," he said.

* * *

On Wednesday morning the Oval Office was empty. The only occupant was President Dean Harding who worked behind his desk. Behind him, the thick windows protected him from any kind of attack.

The Secret Service guards who were usually there to protect the President had been removed from the room. The visitor Harding expected was not considered as dangerous as he had been the Vice President for the last eight years.

Paul Dieckens entered the room and walked to the desk while Harding stood to greet him.

"Paul, thanks for coming. You must be tired."

"Yes. It was a long night."

"I'm sorry I summoned you so early, but we have something important to discuss."

"Sure. Tell me what's up."

Both men sat on the sofas arranged in the office center. Paul Dieckens looked tired. Election Tuesday had been strenuous. National television and radio had covered the event until three in the morning when the results were completed and had made the announcement of the preliminary winner.

"It seems we will finally have to leave the White House."

"Yes, Paul. So, it seems."

"I'm sorry I lost. I'm not sure what happened. Everything looked fine at first. The initial results favored me."

"That's what I wanted to talk to you about, Paul."

"Yes?"

"The truth is that you won the election."

"What? What are you talking about?"

"The results were overwhelming. You should be the next President of the United States."

"I don't understand."

"Yesterday we had an emergency meeting with the Director of the CIA, the FBI and the Attorney General. We agreed that we could not allow a Nazi to occupy the White House."

"What?" The colors left Paul's face.

"We know all about your brother Werner Dietz, that the orphanage where you grew up was run in this country by sympathizers of the regime and that it provided American identifications to the sons of military men and politicians who defected from Germany at the end of the war."

"Who told you all that crap?"

"We have proof, Paul."

Paul knew it was the truth. A sense of frustration overcame him. All the plans he had made with his brother, Werner. Paul Dieckens, upon becoming President was going to propose Germany as a member of the United Nations Security Committee. With the backing of the United States, Germany would again become a superpower. The Gewinn symbol, with a red background with a white circle in the center, would return to its original Nazi flag shape, replacing the letter "G" in the center of the circle with the swastika and filling in the spaces to turn the hand-shaped background into its previous rectangle. All these ideas passed through the mind of the Vice President and a doubt was formed.

"You knew, and even then, you let me continue. Why?"

"We didn't know everything until yesterday. That is why the CIA found itself in the painful situation of altering the electoral results, for the first time in history. But it was the only way to protect the common good."

"Do you know that by telling me this, I can contest the elections?" His mind ran with the possibilities of rescuing the plan in some way.

"Yes, but if you do, you will be exposed for what you are. And I can assure you that not only Israel would be interested in making sure that you suffered an accident."

The intonation of the last word confirmed to Paul Dieckens—Paul Dietz—that although it had been discovered, the information was reserved to only a handful of people.

They were giving him the opportunity to get out of the situation alive without exposing him to public opinion. Although it was shameful for the Harding Administration to admit that they altered the results of an election, the people would understand that this was the lesser of two evils, as the other option was having a Nazi president.

All the plans he had made with his brother, Werner, fell apart. But that was not the last of his surprises.

"Your brother is dead."

"You'd be surprised."

"Not anymore. This time it is true. We even have third-party confirmation."

"How?" Paul could not believe what he was hearing.

"Oscar Brown went to Gewinn's office and found him. I can't go into details, but Werner died while trying to assassinate Oscar.

After a minute of silence, President Harding returned to his desk.

"You're finished, Paul. I don't want to expose you publicly, but I hope you're not fool enough to get involved in any political activity ever again. There are many cases of politicians who disappear from public view after losing an election. You must be one of those cases. That's it. You can retire."

Harding sat behind his desk and resumed reading some documents. At that moment, five Secret Service agents entered through one of the side doors and positioned themselves in different parts of the room.

That was the end, and Paul knew it. Slowly he got up and walked to the door. When he opened it to leave, he hesitated and turned to see the President. His peripheral sight caught three of the agents reaching for their gun. Paul understood the meaning of this action: he was no longer trustworthy.

Paul Dietz left the Oval Office, then left the White House for the last time, being escorted to his vehicle. He observed how the security agents, who until then had overseen protecting him, had been removed from their duties. He understood that, during his conversation with the President, they had been alerted to his new status.

Paul drove off alone.

* * *

Dirk Tromsdorff was an eighteen-year-old who had dropped out of school. This was his first night in his new job in the toilet of the Berlin museum. The pay was not very good, much less the hours. But it was the best he had been able to achieve at that moment.

They had assigned him the war section, and he was sweeping the area when he suddenly stopped in front of a glass box. Inside, on display, was the uniform of the head of World War II, Adolf Hitler.

Dirk could not help feeling admiration for what that uniform represented. Like many Germans, he felt betrayed by the Führer who had lied to them about Aryan supremacy.

Víctor Krieger, his boss, was older than fifty, who had been cleaning the floors of the museum for the past twenty years. He entered the room and observed with a sense of resignation the youth enthralled in front of the glass box. He approached him and, shaking his head, said, "All the rookies end up here the first night."

Dirk turned his attention to him for a moment and continued to admire the uniform. "Can you imagine what would have happened if he had won the war?"

"Do you really think that this is his real uniform?"

"It's not?" Said the apprentice, surprised.

"Of course not! This is some poor devil's uniform! Down in the storage there are hundreds of uniforms and every two years we take one and we add these badges for the exhibition."

CHAPTER TWENTY-FIVE

The international newscasts announced the death of Werner Dietz in his offices on the top floor of Gewinn.

According to the official statement of the Police, Oscar Brown went to the office of Werner Dietz and, when he found him alive, he confronted him about Gewinn's participation in the bankruptcy of the Bank Suisse Corp. They argued. Both being armed made the outcome all the worst in the end. Oscar Brown's assistant alerted the police.

The murder case was closed, but the investigation into the finances of the company would continue for several months.

Another news bulletin reported the discovery of a body washed up by the river. The corpse had been identified as Oscar Brown. He was buried without honors or fanfare in a public graveyard in Frankfurt.

Nora Miller cried for a week after hearing of Oscar's death. Little by little she returned to her work. She thought that if she had once been able to forget Brown when he left her to go to Germany, she could do it now, working sixteen hours a day.

A few months later, just as she was about to get into her car to go home, at nine o'clock at night, she heard a voice calling her.

She turned to see a man in jeans and a Yankee jacket, his face vaguely familiar but she did not know who he was. However, the voice she had heard was that of someone who was dead.

"Nora, I'm Oscar."

She watched him, and she, who knew him well, could not reconcile his look.

"Don't panic. I had plastic surgery. That's why you do not recognize my face. But you do know my voice. You know it's me."

"The news..."

"That was someone else," Brown confirmed. "They said it was me to protect me. I gave them evidence incriminating Gewinn, in exchange for a new life. Now my name is Jason Green. I work as a financial analyst in a consulting firm that works with the government."

"Witness Protection Program," concluded Nora.

"Yes. The FBI helped me."

As an assistant district attorney, Nora knew the procedures of that program very well, having sent a few of her key witnesses in previous cases.

"And what are you doing here? You must cut ties with all your past."

"Yes. That's why I had to wait until now to be able to approach. You see, when we made the deal, I asked for a condition."

"What was it?"

"That they let me rescue something of my past." He paused as he fixed his gaze on the Prosecutor's eyes. "That's something is you."

Nora walked the two steps that separated them and embraced him.

Oscar opened his eyes, turned his head and found that he was the only occupant of the bed. He sat up slowly, walked to the window.

"Always the same dream! Why?"

He left the room and came to the kitchen. The automatic coffee maker had already filled the room with the aromatic scent of fresh brew.

Oscar poured himself a cup and accompanied the drink with a croissant he took out of the oven.

The dream had a brush of reality. His name was now Jason Green, but he did not live in New York, but in Paris, in the apartment that had belonged to his mother. With the help of the FBI, and under his new identity, he made the pertinent procedures through a real estate agency. He had no work and now spent his days walking the streets, feeling a knot in his stomach when he passed in front of a place he had visited with Ruth.

He longed to return to the United States and communicate with Nora. When he took Gewinn's offer and she had stayed, both had put their career above the love they claimed to profess. The blows that Oscar had received afterward had made him change his outlook on life, but he did not believe that Nora had changed. Nor did he believe that the FBI would allow him to approach her. After breakfast, he dressed and left the apartment for an extensive walk around the city. Maybe he'd visit the Louvre. Again.

* * *

Adolf Hoffman emptied the scotch and placed the glass back on the counter. The bartender looked at him and shook his head. No more service for him. That was just as well. How many had he taken, five?

Yes, five. Doubles.

He decided to search for another establishment, one willing to service him more drinks. He'd walk, obviously. The last time he drove he tried to end Oscar Brown's life. It was Oscar Brown. He had hesitated because of the changed hairstyle and new beard. The eyes, however, were a dead giveaway. Oscar had to die. Only dead he'd be useful.

Then at the last second, that secretary had intervened changing fate. Damn that girl.

He got her full on, though.

The look of shock followed by the horror of pain creeping its way through her senses was somewhat as compensation for his failure.

On his way out, he caught Oscar's gaze. Adolf suspected the pair had become a couple. The sad look on Oscar's face confirmed his suspicion.

He drove on. He escaped. He knew he blew it as he'd never see Oscar Brown again.

The man's name had been cleared of all the allegations. The new bad guy was the resurrected Werner Dietz. Although this time he was truly dead. Police crossed their heart on it.

A man without a purpose. He had become a joke, like a rebel without a cause.

Adolf discovered he couldn't walk as soon as he moved from the stool and hit the ground hard. He hit his head against the foot bar at the bottom.

"Damn it!"

A bouncer showed up at his side and helped him to his feet.

The bartender looked horrified. Adolf felt warmth on his face. He touched it and looked at his hand. The crimson mark covered his fingers.

"Time to go home," the bouncer said. "Here, let me walk you out."

The bouncer's tone was gentle but firm. Adolf knew the suggestion was nothing but a command. He was leaving, by his own feet, or walked out by the bouncer. Either way, he was as good as gone.

They didn't even offer to check the cut on his face. They probably didn't have a first aid kit. Adolf let himself be led out. The bouncer didn't drop him in the gutter. The place was upper class after all. Instead, the man hailed a cab and made sure Adolf got in.

"Where to?"

Adolf gave him the address of the small hotel where he had crashed the previous night. He had already gotten rid of the car.

The driver gave the bouncer a thumps-up sign and drove off. The hotel was less than a block away. Easy money for him. Adolf managed to get a few bills from his pocket and paid. The driver didn't help him out, or even make the offer.

Adolf looked at the front door. A man in a brown uniform held the door open for him. He also didn't offer to help. He must look better than he felt. He dragged his feet into the lobby. He had paid the hotel for two nights. He was scrapping the bottom of the barrel. He should not have taken the taxi. Then again, the bouncer didn´t ask or gave him any choice.

He focused on the elevator and made a beeline for it. Halfway across the lobby, his stomach grumbled. He felt bile coming up through his throat. He wouldn't make it to his room. He looked around and found a restroom and ran for it.

He barely made it to the toilet. When he surfaced from the bowl, he saw the trail of nauseating vomit from the door all the way to the stool. His clothes were covered in filth too. For a second, he wondered how he could produce so much bile when he hadn't eaten at all that day.

A man walked into the restroom. He was tall, dressed casually in jeans and a t-shirt. Another guest, Adolf presumed. The man looked at him in disgust. Adolf felt embarrassed, not to have had time to close the stall door.

The man approached. That would be even more embarrassing, receiving help from a stranger in a bathroom. The man stood at the door and looked at all sides, then his gaze centered on Adolf. The man's contempt became visible. Adolf wondered what he had done to earn the stranger's anger.

"The Mossad doesn´t forgive those who attack our agents."

The man pulled out a pistol, pointed at Adolf and pulled the trigger twice. The last thing Adolf saw was the twin flashes from the handgun as it discharged its killing parcels.

* * *

It was an afternoon of nostalgia. Almost at dusk, the sun was tinged in its natural and beautiful yellow color behind the mountains, beyond the horizon, where the peaks cannot be distinguished. The clouds watered throughout the firmament left little to see about their presence on this planet in all their centuries of life.

The borders of the impossible and the infinite combined to show man how small his being is compared to the stars that began to appear behind the clouds; the waters around him seemed to be the perfect culmination for that amazing landscape of nature; the water, the mountains, the sun, the sky, the clouds, the whole universe conspired to offer the best of itself.

His hands trembled with cold, his body shuddered to think about what had happened. It was too late to be left behind, it was impossible to return, and it was useless just thinking about it. His mind no longer worked as it used to. The passage of time had already caused an irremediable effect on him. His body and mind no longer coordinated. It was impossible to return.

His body lying on the shore of the lake in the middle of the night would be easy prey for any animal. But his thoughts wandered through the far corners of the universe, trying to find a way out. He did not understand the impossibility of his desire to recover what he had lost.

The only solution he could think of was suicide, but he was tormented by the question of whether it was the best he could do. The revolver in his hand was the last gift his father had given him before sending him from Germany to the orphanage in the United States.

"Take care of it well. It's the weapon that killed the Führer," he had said.

He took the weapon and aimed it at his head. The bullet would be able to penetrate his temple and blow into a thousand pieces all that it found in its path. His finger on the trigger was ready to squeeze, and end this life, once and for all, with all the suffering that devoured him inside, that did not let him live, that would not let him continue living.

A rumble broke the silence of the panorama. The noise spread quickly through the echo of the mountain. And the whole universe was contracted and darkened by losing one of its members.

But death did not put an end to Paul Dietz's pain. It only prolonged it for the rest of eternity.

THE END

Keep reading for another thrilling adventure featuring The Falcon:

ABSOLUTION
WITHHELD

By J. H. Bográn

ABSOLUTION WITHHELD

A short story featuring The Falcon

By J. H. Bográn

The thief sat inconspicuously in the second row pew when he saw his old friend Daniel Weiss, dressed in the traditional black cassock worn by Roman Catholic priests. The man of God walked towards the confessional, opened the front door of the booth and disappeared inside. *What is he doing here?* Alexander Beck, a.k.a. the Falcon wondered, his thoughts swept away by the sea of memories triggered by the chance sighting of a mere old school chum. As he drummed his fingers on the back of the front pew, he waited in line to take his turn in the confessional. After some time, he entered and knelt.

"Forgive me, Father, for I have sinned." He began with the prayer learned many years before.

The wooden window slid open, the priest's profile visible through the multiple small square holes of the grid.

"Tell me, my son." The voice was soft, benevolent, and still carried the unmistakable London accent.

Alexander lost his voice after the initial exchange. He had come to the church to do a job, not to practice confession of his sins, much less seek absolution. Now he felt his past catching up with him, and quite a past it was for a twenty-three-year-old man. Debating what to share, what to keep secret, he found himself barely able to mumble. It had not been by chance that he took that particular confessional, the third on the row of five positioned on the right side of the ample nave. Perhaps it was divine intervention that, while trying to pry something he had hidden beneath the booth only the night before, he had run into a man he used to know; a man who now happened to be a part of the Church. After a second's hesitation, he sighed and made up his mind.

"I am a sinner," his head down, "I steal from people."

"To steal is a grave sin, my son. Why do you do it?"

"Because I can," he stated in an even tone.

* * *

The night of his hit, Falcon sat on the edge of the single bed inside a nondescript hotel room in the heart of the United Kingdom's capitol. The television set, or telly as the locals called it, flickered every two seconds with the constant thumb clicking of the remote control.

A short double beep on his wristwatch broke his aimless channel surfing. Alex clicked off and stood up, casually dropping the remote on the bed.

He caught his reflection in the mirror: the fake mustache in its proper place although the itching was terrible, his natural jet-black hair now lightened to a dark blonde; his brown eyes hidden under blue contacts. He took a deep breath, squared his shoulders, and left the room.

Falcon covered the distance to the building, to the job. He entered its plush foyer. A solitary guard greeted him from behind the monitoring station.

"Good evening, Mr. Parker. The Christmas party is in full swing."

The real James Parker, tied-up and unconscious under heavy sedation, lay in Falcon's hotel room. The thief felt confident passing the first trial when the guard did not stop him. Still, his response was to flash a knowing smile to the guard while walking past him to the elevator doors on the right. The white cotton undershirt prevented his perspiration from soaking the black silk shirt he wore. He felt self-conscious about the rubber-soled shoes, thinking them out of place, even if they were the same color as his black linen two-piece suit.

The solitary bell announced his ride up had arrived. He stepped in and pushed the button to his destination. On the way up, he stood in the center of the cage, facing his reflection on the polished doors.

"Hi, I'm Parker, James Parker," he practiced then shook his head, "Fool! You won't be introducing yourself to anybody. They know you already."

He got off on his floor, turned left and walked all the way to the last door that stood on the center of the long well-lit heavily-carpeted corridor. The noises from the party managed to escape through the heavy wooden door, indistinct chatter and laughter mixed with Latin rhythms in the background.

"Full swing doesn't quite cover it, does it?"

He stared at the locked door. Affixed to the left wall, almost at chest level, a car reader controlled the entry. The device was similar to the ones used on commercial establishments to swipe credit cards.

Falcon withdrew James Parker's ID card from his inside jacket pocket and swiped it. A bright green light blinked on and, holding his breath, he pushed the door open. Once inside, he was surrounded by the loud music. He stood at the center of the short side of a spacious rectangle. A quartet played on a stage set up at the opposite end. He had studied the building's blueprints and knew the area, now occupied by half-drunk dancing and party-hard employees. The space usually held many secretaries' desks all crammed together.

Wouldn't it have been easier to rent a hall elsewhere instead of moving all the furniture? He shook his head in amazement, although he thanked the managers. Their idea made his job less hazardous. At least, it was easier to a certain degree since there were never any risk-free jobs.

He edged his way through the crowd and the remaining furniture, nodding and smiling at his co-workers, until he reached the base of the stage where the speakers rendered conversation impossible. Parker's office faced the left side of the stage; Falcon found it and entered.

Once inside, he moved around the wooden desk and made a cursory search through all the drawers. Nothing. He perused the walls and lifted each of the four frames. Nothing again. He returned to the chair behind the desk. He cursed his luck, showing the first sign of despair. Were he not to find the information he was hired to retrieve, this entire charade would have been worthless.

His mind raced over the possibilities as his gaze swept the room looking for nooks that might have escaped his first appraisal of the room. Every piece of furniture seemed to be mocking him, the couch by the door, the computer on the desk and the pair of visitor's chairs opposite him. Even the potted plant next to the bathroom door formed a smirk to him.

Sometimes panic gives the kind of clarity that sparks ingenious ideas. Another place to search took form at the front of his mind. He held his breath as he pulled the top drawer all the way out, his hand quickly inspecting the underside. Bingo! He retrieved the gray file folder that Parker had taped there.

Falcon browsed the contents with his penlight. Satisfied, he folded it in half, placed it in his inside jacket pocket, and headed toward the door.

When he was about to reach for the knob, a woman entered the room startling him. She was dressed in a cream silk jacket and matching skirt, a white silk blouse with a red ascot around the collar. Her long black wavy hair hung past her shoulders. She wasted no time putting her arms around his neck, as her caressing tongue parted his lips, probing. Almost stunned, he returned and deepened the kiss until she finally drew back. Her lips were soft, sweet but mixed with traces of alcohol.

"Oh, James! I've been waiting all evening. Why didn't you turn the light on as we agreed?" Her soft voice held no accusatory tone despite her protesting expressions.

"I..." He found himself at a loss for words.

The woman led him backwards through the dark office until he felt the couch behind his knees. She pushed him with her right index finger so he sat down. Without any haste, she removed her wedding band and pocketed it, then unbuttoned her jacket. The darkened office hid her features; still, her silhouette told the tale of a perfectly proportioned body, full breasts that seemed to defy gravity and a rounded derriere. She slipped out of her clothes with playful moves, teasing him, taunting until Falcon felt drunk with desire and ripped off his own garments.

When she drew near, in the nude, Falcon knew he was past the point of no return. He let himself be taken over by the passion of this chance encounter.

Twenty minutes later and dressed again, he heard her stirring on the couch as he grabbed the doorknob.

"I know you're not James," she said.

Falcon's muscles tensed. He turned to face her.

"What are you talking about?" he said forcing a smile.

She extended her hand reaching for her jacket on the table. Rummaging through it until she found what she was looking for. She pulled out a cigarette and lit it. She did not speak again until after she exhaled the first cloud of smoke.

"There's nothing better that a smoke after sex, don't you agree?"

Falcon tilted his head, watching her every move.

"You did a good job copying his hair style, even that annoying part in the middle. It's uncanny! Then, there is the mustache. I think it's a fake. By the way, does it itch too much?" The British accent seemed to envelop every uttered sound in velvet.

Falcon held her gaze feeling she enjoyed toying with him. His pulse ran faster than a few seconds before. His nostrils filling with the smell of her tobacco, the dimmed light partially hid her naked body. He could still taste her kisses, smell her perfume, feel her sweat on his own body.

He felt cornered, thinking of all the ways he could get out of the secured building should she raise the alarm.

"Do you want to know what gave you away?" she taunted.

Falcon grunted.

"First of all, James doesn't have those tight washboard abs," she flashed a smile, "or your vigor. No, he is rather shy in bed. But not you, my dear stranger."

"What do you want?" he said, fearing the worst.

"You already gave me what I wanted," she said laughing then turned serious and added, "The question is: do you have everything you came here for?"

"I don't know what you mean," he said.

"As a security measure, James kept only half of the data here. The rest is in his boss' office across the hall, my husband's. You must go there to get it. On the wall behind his desk hangs a woman's portrait. Look inside the vault hidden underneath."

"Why are you telling me this?"

"Consider it payment for services rendered." She crushed the butt of her cigarette in the ashtray. She rose from the couch, collected her clothes, blew him a kiss, then walked to the bathroom swaying her hips and locked herself in.

Falcon crossed the hall to the other office in the midst of noise. The band, having changed tempo, was now squeaking some rock ballads. He reached the locked door. Thinking he had nothing to lose he tried Parker's magnetic card, shocked with disbelief when the green light went on.

The office was an exact mirror image of Parker's office, the only noticeable difference being the plush executive chair behind the desk.

Falcon rushed around the desk, removed the painting to reveal a small vault. He grimaced eyeing the dial. Perhaps the task would prove complicated and time consuming, but not impossible.

He spotted a glass on top of the desk; he snatched it and placed it next to the dial, cupping the sound. He pressed his ear to the glass and turned the dial clockwise. A soft metallic click stopped him and he reversed direction straining his ear for a similar sound. A full minute and several turns later, a slightly higher click brought a smile to Falcon's face. He held his breath as he turned the handle to open the box. He half expected an alarm but nothing happened. He reached in to grab the sole content: a compact disk.

When he closed the vault door, a piercing alarm filled the office, overpowering the sounds of the band outside. Falcon fled the room knowing that the guard's security panel downstairs must be blinking like a Christmas tree. Having studied the company's security procedures, he knew the guard had already made the call to the police. His chances of escaping unscathed had diminished to a tad above zero.

* * *

"To say you do something simply because you can do it well is a fool's error, Alex."

"You remember me!"

"The moment you spoke, I knew. Are you the one the police came looking for last evening?"

"Yes, Father Daniel. Sorry about that," Falcon said.

"The parish priest had never seen so many officers enter the church at once, especially in the middle of the night. Quite a mess it was! They searched inside the living quarters in the back."

"I was trapped. The church was my only way to escape."

"Men always seek sanctuary in the House of God during desperate times." He paused. "But, why are you here today?"

"I came to retrieve what I left behind." His hand removed a loose panel on the confessional floor and grabbed the folder and compact disk.

Falcon did not know what he had stolen. He knew they were complicated formulas, but that was the extent of his knowledge. To him, getting the information was his mission, for which he received a handsome payment in advance.

"Is that all?"

"At first it was. Now I think fate put you in my path. How else do you explain this?"

Alexander went on to tell Father Daniel all the deeds of his life since they had parted ways after high school graduation. The account took over ten minutes and Father Daniel listened without interruption. Falcon felt like he had just dropped a heavy load. He was nothing even close to a puritan, but telling all his dark secrets to another man had a liberating effect.

"And now you seek forgiveness for these actions?" he asked with benevolence.

"That would mean that I never do it again, wouldn't it?"

"Of course! Don't you remember what Jesus told the woman caught committing adultery?"

"No," Falcon said.

"He said: 'Now go and sin no more.' Are you ready to sin no more?"

Falcon shook his head, unable to respond or even to hold eye contact anymore.

"Alexander, please!" he pleaded.

"I...I can't."

"Then I cannot give you absolution. Your sins are retained until you repent."

Falcon sighed. He had expected such an answer, but that didn't prevent the hurt of actually hearing it said.

"I must go. Will you give me away?"

"No. What you told me is a secret of confession and I cannot betray that trust. I can't condone it either."

"I see. Thank you. Perhaps in a few years..."

"In the line of work you do, you might not live those few years," Daniel cut in.

Falcon's face took on a sad look, a smile contradicted by the eyes which conveyed the lack of joy. He rose and walked down the aisle towards the main doors. At the threshold, he turned to face the line of confessionals. Daniel had exited the booth and stood looking at him.

"There might be something I can do in the meantime," murmured Alexander Beck, the Falcon, as he turned once again and walked out of the church.

THE END

About The Author:

J. H. Bográn is an international author of novels, short stories and scripts for television and film. He's the son of a journalist, but ironically prefers to write fiction rather than facts. His genre of choice is thrillers, but he likes to throw in a twist of romance into the mix.

As a freelance writer, he has several articles published in a wide range of topics. Has also provided English/Spanish translation services as well as simultaneous for events and professional meetings and currently teaches Academic Writing, Public Speaking and English as a Second Language at a local university.

He's a member of The Crime Writers Association, The Author's Guild, the Short Fiction Writers Guild and the International Thriller Writers where he also serves as the Thriller Roundtable Coordinator and contributor editor their official e-zine The Big Thrill.

He lives in Honduras with his wife, three sons, and a Lucky dog.

You can find out more by visiting his website at:

www.jhbogran.com